Lucky Little Things

LET ME Fix THAT FOR YOU

JANICE ERLBAUM

LET ME Fix THAT FOR YOU

Farrar Straus Giroux · New York

Farrar Straus Giroux Books for Young Readers
An imprint of Macmillan Publishing Group, LLC
120 Broadway, New York, NY 10271

Printed in the United States of America by
LSC Communications, Harrisonburg, Virginia
Designed by Aimee Fleck
First edition, 2019

1   3   5   7   9   10   8   6   4   2

mackids.com

Library of Congress Control Number: 2018027810

ISBN 978-0-374-30810-0

Our books may be purchased in bulk for promotional, educational, or business
use. Please contact your local bookseller or the Macmillan Corporate and
Premium Sales Department at (800) 221-7945 ext. 5442 or by email at
MacmillanSpecialMarkets@macmillan.com.

For my dad

LET ME FIX THAT FOR YOU

1

Monday Lunch

I am sitting in the cafeteria at school on a Monday, minding my business.

And I've got *a lot* of business to mind.

"Hey, girl." Sophie Nelson, vice president of the seventh-grade student council, slides into the newly empty seat next to mine and puts her hand on my arm, as though we're friends. "I have a favor to ask . . ."

Taye, our class's designated Hot Guy, has been standing in front of my table. When Sophie sits down, he crosses his arms over his chest and glowers at her. "Uh, Sophie?" he says. "I was waiting . . ."

"Hurry up," urges Jasmine, band geek, standing behind Taye. "There's other people waiting, too."

Business is always brisk on Mondays. Fridays, too—there's the rush before the weekend, then there's the rush afterward. Midweek, I'm eating lunch alone, or with Harry Homework, who's on the same schedule as me: super-popular on Mondays and Fridays, yeah-whatever the rest of the time. Looking to my left, I see Harry's line is as long as mine. Why can't anybody need a favor on a Tuesday?

We've got to move this crowd along, or Ms. Schellestede's going to notice. Out of the three people in front of me, I like Jasmine the best, and I want Sophie to like me the most.

But Taye has the next spot in line, and I'm curious what he has to say.

"What do you need?" I ask him.

Sophie and Jasmine roll their eyes and move a few feet away, as Taye sits down in the spot Sophie just left. He puts his backpack on the table in front of us and scoots closer to me so we're (mostly) blocked from view.

"Hurry," Jasmine insists. "We only have ten minutes left."

Ten minutes left for lunch, and I haven't eaten half of the hummus sandwich I made this morning. I pick it up and take a huge bite, alfalfa sprouts falling like shriveled four-leaf clovers in my lap.

Taye drops his voice to a murmur. "I need you to slip this box of chocolates into someone's bag."

Ooh! Taye has a crush. From the front pocket of his backpack, he removes a small square box. There're maybe four chocolates in there, but they're the really good kind, you can tell from the box. It's glossy bronze with a purple ribbon and surprisingly hefty in my hand as we make the transfer. I wouldn't mind if somebody gave me a box of chocolates like that, and I allow myself a brief fantasy where I'm Taye's crush before I snap back to reality and stash the box in my bag.

My first question: "Who?"

Taye cups his hand over his mouth and whispers a name. I'm surprised, but I don't show it. I keep my face and voice neutral as I ask the rest of the basic questions: *What* does the bag look like? *When* does Taye want it done? *Where* does the Target go after lunch?

I don't ask him *How*. The *How* is up to me. And the one question I never ask a client is *Why*.

Taye fills me in and I confirm the details, but he still looks nervous. "You won't tell anybody, right? I don't want them to know it's from me."

"No way." I take my position very seriously. For me, being a problem-fixer is like being a priest, or a therapist—anything you tell me is confidential. I remind Taye of my pledge: "I know nothing, I remember nothing, and I delete everything."

Taye's face relaxes and he grabs his pack and rises to leave. "You're the best," he says, shooting me with finger guns as he departs. "I owe you one."

I wave Jasmine over, and she takes the seat Taye

vacated. She's practically chewing through her lower lip with anxiety.

"I need an excuse," she says quickly. "Like, right away."

Jasmine explains that she skipped band practice last week. Which is weird, because Jasmine loves playing the drums. Every teacher in our grade has a drawerful of drumsticks, chopsticks, pens, paintbrushes, and rulers they've confiscated to stop Jasmine from drumming in class. I wonder why she would purposely skip band. But I don't need to know her reasons for skipping band. I just have to solve her problem.

I quickly review the classic excuse options:

1. Illness/personal injury
2. Family tragedy
3. Transportation woes
4. Other appointment

Options one through three have been used on teachers since school was invented, so we'll go with the rarest and the finest: other appointment. But not a dentist or doctor's appointment—Jasmine doesn't have a note.

Jasmine's leg jiggles and Sophie makes little frustrated grunting noises from her spot a few feet away. I know they want me to hurry, but I can't just pull something out of thin air. That's not how I work.

Here's how I work: I concentrate on our music/band teacher, Mr. Gerber. Gerber used to play bass guitar in a real rock band, before he had kids, and he still wears one earring and a leather jacket. He tries to be the "cool teacher," saying things like, *It's lit up in here*, or *Hashtag goals*, while everyone sits there quietly burning to a crisp with the embarrassment he's too clueless to feel. What Gerber wants more than anything is for kids to think of him as a friend.

Aha.

"Okay," I begin, as Jasmine looks at me eagerly. "You were auditioning for a garage band some high school kids are starting. But your mom's against you joining the band, so you didn't tell her about the audition, so she didn't write you a note. And Gerber can't call your mom to check your excuse or he'll get you in trouble and ruin your chance to be in the band."

Jasmine's jaw drops so far, the rubber bands around her braces nearly fly off and ricochet around the room. "That's . . . that's perfect," she says gratefully. "You're incredible. Thanks, G. I owe you one."

"No problem," I say, and I actually mean it. I enjoy doing things for people I like, and I glow with the satisfaction of a job well done. Jasmine jumps up from her chair and dashes off to deliver this freshly baked excuse to Mr. Gerber.

Immediately, Sophie takes over the seat. I bite into my sandwich and motion for her to begin.

"So this favor . . . ," says Sophie. "It's not really a favor for me? It's more for a friend."

Asking for a friend. LOL. As much as I would like

to believe that one of Perfect Sophie Nelson's snobby friends needs my help, I know better. Of course the "friend" Sophie is talking about is herself, but I'm not going to force her to admit that.

Sophie continues, "So . . . my friend, she borrowed something, and she has to give it back."

Uh-oh. This is the second time Sophie's come to me because one of her "friends" needed to replace or return something. Not coincidentally, this is the second time Sophie has talked to me.

Last month was the first time. Liz Kotlinski's silk scarf went missing, and Liz was threatening to personally search every single student's locker and bag until she found it. Sophie had grabbed me in a panic between classes—"Hey, I need your help"—then thrust a paper bag containing the scarf at me. Apparently, one of Sophie's "friends" had taken the scarf "by mistake," but neither Sophie nor her "friend" wanted to be the one to return it to Liz, because "it might look weird."

I call these jobs "reverse retrievals."

I nod in understanding and motion for Sophie to hurry up and get on with it. Kids around us have started packing up and throwing away their trash; we don't have time for her stalling. "What can I do for your friend?"

Sophie cringes like she'd rather not say. I notice her flawlessly manicured nails digging into the palms of her hands. She leans in and whispers in my ear.

I have a hard time keeping a straight face when I hear her request. Sophie's not making a life-or-death request, but what she's asking is nearly impossible.

Sophie needs a *big, big* favor.

2

The Present
(and the Past)

I'm Glad.

Go ahead, get it out of your system:

"*Glad* to meet you!"

"Well, I'm happy, too!"

"What are you so *Glad* about?"

Etc. These are just the top three. I have heard infinite variations on the joke that is my name. Yours will not amuse me.

Yes, my name is Glad. It's short for Gladys. This was my mom's idea. She named all three of us girls: I'm Gladys, my older sister is Mabel, and my younger sister is Agnes. If we'd been boys, Dad would have named us—that was Mom and Dad's bargain—and we might have semi-normal names. But Mom has always been pretty artistic, so of course we had to have quirky names. Which leads to quirky nicknames. For as long as I can remember, people have called me Glad, and they call my big sister Mabey. They call my little sister Agnes, because Agnes refuses to answer to a nickname. She's only nine years old and three and a half feet tall, but Agnes doesn't let anybody talk down to her.

Agnes is probably my favorite person these days. She's so curious and enthusiastic about the world, in that innocent way little kids get to be before they hit middle school and have to start pretending that everything is boring and stupid. She's always excited to tell me things she learned that day: "I watched this *incredible* video of a sea horse having babies—it looked like there was a hundred of them, exploding out of the father's pouch—did you know that male sea horses carry the babies?"

Agnes is literally a genius. She's going to be a

scientist—actually, she's already started being one, since Dad bought her a chemistry set and helped her create a small lab in the basement. Now Agnes spends most of her time in her basement lab, instead of in our shared bedroom, which feels much bigger and emptier when she's not around.

Actually, the whole house feels big and empty. Mabey's always upstairs in her attic room, listening to early '00s emo and taking comments on famous people's Instagrams very personally. Dad's always at his boring job (tax lawyer). And Mom's been staying with a bunch of her old college friends on a communal farm in New Mexico, a ten-hour drive away, to "get her head together."

Mom was only supposed to be gone a few weeks—a "trial separation" Dad called it on that fateful night when they gathered us girls in the living room and gave us the terrible news. "Two or three months, at most."

A year and a half later, she hasn't come back. Not even for a visit. She was going to come home for a visit around Thanksgiving last year, but then she and Dad got in a fight and she canceled. Dad doesn't know it, but I still haven't forgiven him for that.

If I met a genie, I'd ask for Mom to come home first, and *then* I'd ask for billions of dollars and world peace. I keep hoping she's going to come through the door and scoop me up and tickle-hug me, the way she always did. Then I'd follow her upstairs and sit on the bed while she changed into her house sweats and told me about the funny thing that happened that day.

Because Mom can make anything funny. The stupidest show on TV becomes the most entertaining when she comments along with it. "Is the lead guy supposed to be handsome? He kind of looks like a thumb with eyebrows."

And she wasn't just funny, she was *fun*. If Dad wasn't home, she'd let us run around the house and jump on the furniture, or eat ice cream before dinner, or any of the seventy-five other things Dad didn't want us doing. And she was exciting. Like the time she took me and Agnes to a movie at the multiplex, and we got bored with the movie we were watching, so she sneaked us into another theater, where the movie was PG-13, and we spent the whole time giggling over what we got away with.

Funny story: Mom is the first person I ever fixed for. I was nine years old, Mabey was thirteen, and Agnes was six. Even at age six, Agnes was way too smart for the rest of the family, and she needed constant supervision so she didn't do things like pour baking soda and vinegar into the toilet to make a toilet volcano (note: kind of disgusting, but also kind of awesome). Keeping her out of trouble was an ongoing struggle for Mom.

Since Dad's career in tax law paid money and Mom's career in making lopsided pottery didn't, Dad kept working and Mom took care of us kids. She drove us places and kept the fridge reasonably stocked and made sure we bathed every so often. She packed our lunches in the morning and picked us up from school. Sometimes she complained about being "just a stay-at-home mom," and about how much of her "authentic, creative self" she had given up to be a mother, and about how badly she needed an identity of her own. She could get lost in her thoughts at times, and she'd get grouchy if we interrupted and brought her back down to earth. But we always knew that Mom was there for us.

Until she wasn't.

It started when Agnes began kindergarten. All of a sudden, Mom had her days free, and she wanted to go back to making pottery at the studio in town, but Dad wanted her to get a paying job. I eavesdropped on several of their arguments (not hard, since they were shouting), and they all boiled down to three things:

1. Dad was tired of being the sole breadwinner for our family of five.
2. Dad wanted Mom to contribute more to the household and be less flaky.

3. Dad was an uptight, condescending @&%#! who was murdering Mom's free spirit with his conformist, middle-class values.

But none of this was new. Mom and Dad were always kind of an "opposites attract" couple. They just didn't used to fight about it so much.

One day, about a year into these tense times, when Agnes had just started first grade, I came through the door from a day at school and my mother instantly pounced on me. I noticed that she was still wearing her clay-covered pottery jeans instead of her at-home sweatpants. Mom must have walked in the door just minutes before I did.

"Gladdy, I need your help. I made a mistake, and I need you to help me fix it."

I nodded yes right away, delighted to be singled out by Mom for one-on-one attention. As the middle child, I've often felt like the odd one out. Mabey is so much like Mom, dramatic and emotional and forgetful, with those big brown eyes and long lashes. And Agnes is a little female version of logical, dorky Dad, down to the light sprinkling of freckles on her cheeks. But I'm nobody's child, with a personality and looks that came from nowhere. I'm like a bunch of random Legos someone mooshed together before saying, "Here, it's a person."

I followed Mom into the kitchen. We sat down at the table, and she pulled her chair close to mine.

Mom spoke quickly, nervously playing with one of her earrings. "I was a little bit late picking up Agnes from school today. I left the studio on time, but there was so much traffic, and . . . all sorts of commotion, and I wasn't able to get there when I said I would."

She sounded so guilty and upset. "That's not your fault," I said, trying to console her.

"And my phone was dead," Mom continued. "So I couldn't call the school and tell them I was on the way, and they couldn't get in touch with me. It was *so* frustrating."

Stupid phone, I thought. *Poor Mom.*

"And your father was supposed to give the school his new phone number, but he forgot. He gave everybody in the world his new number, except the school. So they couldn't reach him, either."

Dad forgot to give the school his new number! And he calls Mom irresponsible! A few weeks before, Dad had started getting a million calls for someone named Speedy, who was in demand with some very angry people, so Dad ditched the number and got a new one. And he forgot to tell the school!

But the most important thing was Agnes. "Is Agnes okay?"

"Well . . . ," Mom said. She gestured to say *so-so.* "She wasn't happy about waiting around. She wouldn't talk to me when I got there, and then she fell asleep in the car. I put her up in your room."

Of course Agnes wasn't happy. Any six-year-old would be unhappy waiting around after school, not knowing when their mom is coming to pick them up, with no way to reach her. It was especially bad for Agnes, who thrived on routine. I stood, ready to go upstairs and comfort her.

Mom gestured for me to sit again, so I did. "Before you go up there . . . See, this is where I need your help. We need to make sure Agnes doesn't tell your father what happened."

I frowned. "But it was his fault, because of his phone number."

Mom shook her head. "He won't see it that way. I just know he'll find a way to blame me, and I don't want another argument. It would be great if we could keep Agnes from saying anything." She looked at me pleadingly and softened her voice. "You have such a terrific imagination and you're so good at solving puzzles. Can't you think of something, honey?"

I must have turned pink with pride. Mom needed my help! I loved being helpful, unless it involved cleaning the house. I would not fail Mom. I concentrated my terrific imagination on Agnes.

My sister, my roommate, with her restless little feet that kicked at her blankets when she slept . . .

Aha.

"What if it was a dream?" I asked.

Mom looked at me skeptically. "What do you mean?"

"What if Agnes dreamed that it happened and thought it was real?"

Agnes, brilliant though she was, was also young enough to get confused about what was a dream and what was real. If she saw a movie one day, she might tell you the next day about the dream she'd had and then recount the entire plot of *Finding Nemo.* One recent morning, we were eating breakfast in the kitchen, and Agnes started yelling, "This is a dream! I have dreamed this all before!" It took about a half hour to explain that she was having déjà vu, and even then, she wasn't fully convinced she was awake.

Mom drew back slowly and regarded me with admiration. "Gladdy," she said. "That is *good.*"

Aw, shucks.

I looked down bashfully, but I was glowing with pleasure. Compliments are like chocolate chip cookies—you can never get too many.

Mom rose from her seat and started pacing. "Right. Agnes had a bad day at school, and then she fell asleep in the car, so I carried her up to bed, and she had a bad dream, but she thought it was real. Brilliant!"

She beamed at me and kissed me on the head, then ran to her bedroom to change her clothes before Dad got home. I went upstairs to our bedroom to see how my little sister was doing and try to convince her when she woke up that her upsetting reality had been just a dream.

Looking back on it now, I feel terrible that I lied to Agnes. I remember how frustrated she was that afternoon, insisting that it had happened, Mom forgot her at school, it wasn't a dream, while I told her over and over that she was mistaken. That's a messed-up thing to do to somebody. I'll have to think of a way to make it up to her.

At the time, though, I didn't think I was doing

anything wrong. I didn't particularly enjoy watching Mom lie to Dad at the dinner table that night, while Agnes pouted upstairs because nobody believed her true story. But I had to keep Mom and Dad from fighting, and it worked.

I wanted to be Mom's helper and make her happy. I tried to keep her and Dad together in harmony. I used every bit of my great imagination and puzzle-solving skills to make that happen, but it wasn't good enough.

Mom still left.

Last time I spoke to Mom was about a week ago. I was sitting on my bed, picking at the leftover polish on my toenails, trying to picture what Mom was doing on her side of the phone. I could hear a sink running on and off in the background, people talking, a dog barking. She was telling me about the kiln they'd built on the farm, and how she wanted to expand it into a whole ceramics studio. "Besides the money we could make, it's such a physical, creative exercise, you know? So primal."

"When are you coming home?" I asked.

Mom stopped short at my blunt interruption, and I held my breath. Questions like this always upset Mom, and I didn't want her to start crying—nothing feels worse than making Mom cry. But I couldn't stop myself from asking.

She sighed. "I miss you, too," she said sadly. "This is also hard for me, you know?"

That wasn't exactly an answer to my question. "So come home."

This time, her sigh sounded a little impatient. "It's not that simple, BunBun. I mean, the timing . . . It's been very busy here, all the animals decided to give birth at the same time, and I've been up to my ears in baby chicks. They're so cute, you would love them—"

I cut her off. "But we really miss you. All of us do."

There was a long pause. I held my breath. I'd messed up, I'd upset Mom—I was pushing her too hard, and she hated being pushed. But her voice was gentle when she finally spoke. "Honey, you know I miss you girls so much. I wish this was easier for everyone. But the longer I've been here, the more I realize that your father and I . . . Oh, never mind. I shouldn't be talking to you about this stuff."

"Dad can change," I said.

Mom scoffed, "He's not changing. He wants *me* to change. And I tried for years, BunBun, but I was getting to the point where I just didn't recognize myself anymore . . ."

I knew the rest of this speech. She'd been lost, and she needed to find herself. She couldn't be a good mother until she became a full person. She would only be at the farm a little bit longer. She would come visit soon, she just had to figure out the timing.

"BunBun. Please. Please understand how much I miss you, and how much I want to work things out. I just need a little bit longer here. I promise I'll come see you as soon as I can. Maybe in a few weeks, when the timing is better . . ."

I am so sick of the stupid timing.

Since that last phone call, I've been racking my brain for a plan to get Mom home for good. Like, what if there was an emergency? What if I pretended to get really sick? No, Dad would just take me to the doctor, and they'd figure out that I was faking it. What if Agnes blew up the house? No, then there'd be no home for Mom to come back to. What if . . .

I'm glad I'm not one of my clients, because I got nothing. No scheme, no story, no luck. It worries me. As much as I don't want to admit it, I know from watching other people's mistakes that some things can't be fixed.

What if our family is one?

3

Monday Afternoon

Fixers don't have a lot of friends.

I wish I'd known that was part of the deal. The whole reason I got into the fixing game was to make friends. I never really fit in at my old school—I wore the wrong brands and liked the wrong things, so I mainly hung out with the other nobodies. I was hoping that would change when we moved to be closer to Dad's work and I was enrolled here at Elmhaven, but I transferred in the middle of sixth grade and everybody was all paired up already. Nobody needed a spare friend, especially not a weird new girl with a stupid name. "Try getting involved with an activity," Dad suggested, seemingly forgetting that I have no special talents or hobbies and I'm no good at sports. So I thought maybe I could help people with their problems, and that would make them like me.

Well, people have been helped. People still don't like me. These are facts.

I mean, nobody *hates* me. I don't get picked on, like some kids, and I'm grateful for that. Nobody even teases me. Maybe they're afraid of what I might say in return. I've never broken my "I know nothing, I remember nothing, and I delete everything" policy, but they don't know that. Why would they risk me opening my mouth?

At this point, I'd almost rather be teased than ignored. Nobody says mean things to me, but nobody says anything nice to me, either. I don't get invited to sit with people at lunch. People don't say hi in the halls. I walk out of school at the end of the day with everybody else, but I still feel totally alone.

I scan the various clusters of kids standing

together outside. There's Olivia Kurtzweil, who lost her retainer last week and came to me for help. "I already lost two this year," she pleaded. "My parents are going to take my phone if I lose another one." I didn't find it, but I did tell her how to replace it: "Grab someone's old retainer from the Lost and Found, stomp on it, then tell your parents it fell on the ground and got crushed by someone when you took it out of your mouth at lunch. A broken retainer is better than no retainer. You'll still need a new one, but this way it's not your fault."

Olivia sees me looking in her direction, gives me the shortest of smiles, and turns away.

Over by the benches there's Damien Ng. On Valentine's Day, Damien asked me to tell someone he liked them—my favorite kind of job. Unfortunately, that someone didn't like Damien in return, and I had to go back and break the bad news to him—my least favorite kind of job. So Damien got mad at *me*, like somehow it was my fault, and now he ignores me entirely.

Bethany Bond stands alone on the sidewalk. Bethany came to me last month with a problem: She left her phone unlocked around the wrong people, who forwarded certain messages to other people, who definitely should not have seen them. As a result, Bethany lost two friends, a crush, and her trust in humankind. I tried to be nice about it when she told me the problem and asked for my help, but part of me was like, *What do you want me to do for you here? Hypnotize everyone into amnesia?* I told her I was sorry, but I didn't see a way to make the situation better. And Bethany told me she *wasn't* sorry, but I was a terrible, selfish person for not doing anything to help her.

Sometimes I wish I'd stuck to fixing things at home—covering for Mabey when she went through her vaping phase, convincing Dad that Agnes wasn't using the barbecue lighter as a blowtorch. I thought that sharing my gift at school would make me popular, but it had the opposite effect. And what am I going to do about it now? Stop helping people who need it? It's the only thing I'm really good at.

Madison Graham gives me a nervous look as I pass her standing with her friends Violet and Vanessa. At least I understand why Madison doesn't say hi to me—our business is ongoing and confidential. Last week, she asked me to help prove to her friends that she really *does* have a boyfriend in Canada—the fake social media accounts she made aren't enough anymore. She needs texts, and she needs to get them when she's with her friends. So my number is now in her phone as "James," with a picture of a handsome boy with a tight fade, and this morning I texted her a good-morning medley of kissy-kissy emojis.

"Hey, Glad."

"*Bagawk.*" I'm startled into making a noise like a defective emu. While I was busy moping about how nobody says hi to me, Hot Guy Taye snuck up behind me and whispered my name. Which is not okay. Like, I understand you want to be hush-hush about talking to me, but I can't help you if I'm dead from shock.

"Did you . . . deliver the package?" he whispers.

"Done," I report. Easy as one, two, three:

1. I put the fancy box of chocolates in a plain paper bag for ease of transfer. That box was too noticeable to carry undisguised.
2. I waited until just before seventh period, when the Target was socializing over at someone else's desk, leaving their backpack open and unattended on their seat.
3. I walked by their desk and discreetly dumped the box from its paper bag directly into the backpack.

Taye anxiously looks over at the Target, standing a few yards away with their mutual friends. "And nobody saw you?"

Okay, there's a *very* small chance that Taye's friend Jackson saw me make the transfer out of the corner of his eye, but I'm not sure. Jackson didn't look right at me, and he didn't say anything about it to me, so I figure we're safe. "No one," I assure Taye.

He keeps his eyes on his group of friends and frowns. "I was kind of hoping for a response."

I shrug. That's not my department. "You sent them anonymously."

"Could you maybe find out—" he starts, when Liz Kotlinski shouts to him from their cluster.

"Taye!"

Liz waves, and Taye waves back. "Gotta go," he mumbles, then jogs away to join his friends and probably scramble to explain why he was talking to me. Because everybody knows, the only reason to talk to Glad the Fixer is when you need something fixed.

I head toward my bus. Taye is now with his group, standing next to the Target. He doesn't acknowledge me as I pass.

As usual, I'm one of the first people on the bus.

I take a seat near the front. Through the window, I see everyone else hanging out with their friends, laughing and yelling, totally carefree. Even Perfect Sophie Nelson is giggling with her dance squad girls, no trace of the trouble she's in on her face.

Bye, Olivia. Bye, Damien. Bye, Bethany. Bye, Madison. Bye, Sophie.

All in a day's work.

4

Tuesday Morning

I am silently studying Dad at the breakfast table.

Dad is now the focus of my astounding fixing powers. I'm going to get him to change his ways so that Mom will want to come home. Of course, he doesn't know about my plan—he doesn't even know my powers exist. For someone who went to school for so many years, Dad doesn't know about a lot of things.

Correction: Dad knows about a lot of *things*, but he doesn't know very much about *people*. Look at him now, reading his tablet and slurping his coffee, oblivious to his daughters, who wince with every slurp. Mom hated his slurping, and Mabey and I learned to hate it, too, but Dad says that slurping helps cool the coffee on the way to his mouth so it doesn't burn his tongue. Everything Dad does is great with Agnes, so she doesn't mind.

We'll have to fix the slurping.

"Mmm, Agnes," Dad says absentmindedly. "Baxter is picking you up after chess today."

"Okay," she says. "Can he take me to the hardware store on the way home?"

See, now, this is exactly the type of thing Dad needs to notice. Certainly he's aware that Agnes + hardware store = mayhem in the basement. But Dad just slurps his coffee, eyes on his tablet, and says, "Sure."

Baxter, BTW, is Agnes's babysitter. Dad pays him to pick up Agnes from school most days, and even though Mabey is there to "watch" us in the afternoons, Baxter often sticks around until dinner, doing college coursework at the kitchen table or playing a game with Agnes. Sometimes he even stays to eat with us. Baxter is a giant nerd (literally giant—he's nearly seven feet tall, and he has to get his enormous shoes from a specialty store that caters to basketball players and clowns), but I kind of don't mind having him around after school, especially when Mabey brings her high school friends home.

Mabey rolls her eyes. "Can you tell Baxter he doesn't need to, like, hang around when Agnes gets home? He drops off Agnes, and then he stays all day. People are like, 'Oh, who's that, your nanny?' I'm almost seventeen, I could be a camp counselor this summer! I don't need a sitter. It's embarrassing."

Dad looks at Mabey over the top of his tablet. He does this thing where he just looks at you without speaking, tilting his head a little, like he's honestly curious about exactly what kind of life-form you are. Then he waits for you to get so nervous that you blurt out something incriminating. I call it his Lawyer Look, and I hate being on the other end of it.

Mabey rolls her eyes again. "What are you looking at?" she asks rudely, but Dad doesn't answer. He just keeps looking at her with mild interest.

"People," he says finally. "People ask you about Baxter."

She and I both realize her mistake at the same time.

"Who are these people?" he asks calmly. "And what are they doing in my house?"

Mabey's face turns red. "It's my house, too!" she yells. She flings one arm in my direction. "It's Glad's and Agnes's house, too! You're not the only one who lives here! God!"

Dad's famous smile appears, the tiny one that drove Mom crazy. "*Pretty* sure my name is on the deed here. *Pretty* sure I've been paying the mortgage and taxes and upkeep for the past two years."

We'll have to fix this tone of voice. And the tiny smile.

"So what? Just because we don't pay rent, we don't get any rights?"

The infuriating smile gets bigger and Dad's eyebrows raise. "I will answer your question after you answer mine."

"People! Just, like . . . classmates!" She chugs the rest of her juice and gets up to slam her dishes into the dishwasher. "You should be happy at least one of your daughters has friends."

Mabey storms out of the kitchen into the hall. We hear her quickly gathering her things, then the front door bangs shut behind her.

"I have friends," says Agnes, offended.

"Me too," I add quickly.

Kind of.

Agnes goes upstairs, and I head into the hall to get my stuff together for the day. When I go back into the kitchen to say bye, Dad isn't smiling anymore. He's not looking at his tablet. He's staring at a spot on the wall. He doesn't look happy.

I bet he's thinking about Mom. I bet he wishes Mom was here to talk to Mabey, and to pick up Agnes from school, and to pack lunches for us so we don't have to make our own, which is especially hard when you don't know what's going to be in the fridge on any given day, because nobody actually grocery shops anymore, and you are so dead freakin' tired of takeout and pizza and Chinese food every night, and you're lucky that Mabey occasionally makes a list of things for Dad to get, because he's still not used to grocery shopping, and otherwise you would have no toilet paper.

Or maybe that's just me.

No, I know Dad misses Mom. I know he still loves her. He doesn't ever talk about it, but I remember how it was between them, long ago, when I was a little kid. I remember how they danced with me and Mabey in the living room to the Wiggles; how he would say *smooch* right before he kissed her, and she would say *smooch* right after. They used to pat each other on the butt all the time. It was beyond disgusting.

Dad wants Mom home as much as the rest of us, I know it. He's just too stubborn to do anything about it. Which means I'm going to have to do some major scheming if I want to make this family work again. But at least I know where to begin—I'll figure out the rest as I go along.

Step one: Fix Dad.

5

Tuesday Lunch

Today's to-do list is pretty long:

- Madison Graham needs me to send some more texts from James the Fake Canadian Boyfriend.

- Rebecca Lewis needs me to spread a new nickname for her, so people won't keep calling her Becky. She wants people to call her Rebba. I'm not sure that's better.

- Taye needs me to slip an anonymous note into the Target's bag. I tried to tell Taye that he's not going to get the response he wants if the Target doesn't know who to respond to. But NMB = NMP (not my business = not my problem).

- Sam Boyd needs me to keep Evelyn Ferszt from smacking the teeth out of his head after she got busted cheating off his math test. "I don't know how this is my fault," he complained to me nervously. "But you gotta help me fix this. I'm too young for dentures."

- Sophie Nelson needs . . . a miracle.

- I need a break.

Tuesday lunch is usually a good time for me to look over my open accounts. It's just me and Harry Homework at our table today. Nobody's waiting to speak to either of us, which is lucky. I have too many unfinished jobs right now, and I can't afford to disappoint a client and lose a potential friend. Harry flips through his notebook and munches on his usual lunch of oily sardines in a tin. "High protein," he says. "Good for brain development." I try not to gag at the smell/sight/thought.

Harry is the closest thing I have to a real friend here at Elmhaven Middle School. Like Agnes, Harry is a pint-size genius—he's only ten, because he skipped two grades already, and he should probably skip the rest and go straight to, like, Brain Surgeon School or Astronaut Academy, but his mother doesn't want him to skip any more grades because it would "ruin his social life."

Haaaaaaaa!

She doesn't want to *ruin* his *social life*. His social life, which consists of sitting in the back corner of the lunchroom with Glad the Fixer, selling homework so he doesn't get beat up or harassed by older kids. Because nobody really cares what André the Anti-Bullying Aardvark has to say about befriending kids with differences. The only thing keeping Russell Sharpe and the other eighth graders from permanently stuffing Harry into a locker is Harry's homework business.

"Heads up," Harry mutters to me.

I'm about to ask why when I see Ms. Schellestede coming our way. Tall, gray-haired, and imposing, Ms. Schellestede is our school's vice principal, our grade's guidance counselor, and my personal walking nightmare.

"Gladys," says my nightmare, approaching the table. "And Harrison."

Ms. Schellestede makes the kind of eye contact that burns through your eyeballs all the way to the back of your skull. You try not to look, but her stare is like a tractor beam from an alien spacecraft. If you get caught in it, there's no escape. You're going to the spaceship to get probed.

"Well," says Schellestede probingly, as Harry and I look down at the table. "I see we're eating our lunch undisturbed today. As opposed to yesterday, when you were both so popular."

There is a long pause while we try to figure out how to answer this. "Tweens," says Harry, venturing a look up at her. "They're so fickle."

"Yeah," I say. I force a weak smile. "One day you're in, the next day you're out."

Ms. Schellestede gives us a raised eyebrow. She was not born yesterday. She wasn't even born this century. "As I recall, we have talked about this. Both of you have been in my office to discuss your 'businesses,' and both of you were warned to stop plying your trades immediately."

Okay, these are facts.

About six weeks ago, Schellestede called me into her office, tractor-beamed me with her eyes, and told me she knew what I was up to. She knew I had helped Saffron Navinder come up with a way to get out of gym (she faked having terrible balance). She knew I came up with Kathy Park's excuse for not having her history report (she got so interested in the topic that she kept reading about it, so she fell behind on writing about it). She knew I was behind Rafe Sotomayor's explanation for disrupting assembly (he thought he saw lice crawling on the back of the seat in front of him). There was no proof and no way Schellestede could have known those things for sure, so I confessed to nothing. She threatened me with detention anyway.

"But . . . I didn't do anything. I didn't break any school rules," I protested, incredulous.

Schellestede's eyes narrowed, focusing her glare into two sizzling lasers aimed directly at my face. "I'm charging you with 'accessory to lying.'"

Harry was called into her office right after me, and he got it even worse than I did. Schellestede said she knew he was helping people to cheat and plagiarize, and if he got caught in the act, he could be expelled. He had to do some advanced lawyer-type negotiating to keep her from dropping the hammer on him right then and there, pointing out that he didn't do assignments for other students, he simply "gave them the resources to help them complete their assignments in a timely manner." Which is true. Harry won't write your report for you. He'll just provide you with an outline. A single-spaced, page-and-a-half-long outline.

Now Harry opens his mouth to do more lawyering, but Schellestede turns on him with the Stare and he wilts. She puts both hands on the table and leans toward us. We shrink back in our seats.

"If I see a line of people at your table again," she says, enunciating every word, "you had *best* be selling lemonade."

She continues the Stare for another minute. It is the longest minute in the history of time. It is seriously like an hour-long minute. Clocks around the world get annoyed and walk off the job. We all grow long Rip Van Winkle beards that dry up and fall off our faces. This minute will never end, and we will never be released from Schellestede's deadly gaze.

Harry and I are frozen silent until Schellestede takes her hands off the table, straightens up, and walks away. She is halfway across the cafeteria before we exhale.

"What do we do now?" I ask.

"I don't know," says Harry. "Quit?"

I know he's not seriously suggesting that we quit. I can't quit—people need me. And I need them to need me. "I can't quit," I confess.

"I know." He slumps in his chair. "I can't, either. But I think about it sometimes. I'm so sick of trying to find something new for people to say about Shirley Jackson's 'The Lottery.' It's an allegory for the desperate brutality of society under capitalism! The end!"

(I laugh, but that's a freebie, and I'm writing it down.)

I don't know. Maybe quitting would be a relief. I could throw my to-do list of favors into the trash. Let Madison Graham write her own fake texts from her fake boyfriend. Let Evelyn Ferszt pound Sam Boyd into next week. Let me just live my life. But (a) I'm not sure I have a life outside of fixing, and (b) if I quit, everybody will be mad at me for letting them down. I can't let that happen.

So when this girl Izzy comes toward our table, even though Schellestede is still in eyeshot, I don't turn her away. Tuesday favors are usually urgent, and Izzy looks fully upset.

"Hey, Izzy!" I crow loudly as she approaches, winking at her like I'm trying to take flight using only the lashes of my right eye. "Thank you for offering to help me with my . . . soccer playing! I can't wait to discuss it some more! Why don't you walk with me to my locker?"

Izzy frowns for a second, trying to remember when in her life she ever promised to help me with soccer. Then she sees the demented winking and gets it. "Uh, yeah, sure," she says. "Soccer."

I grab my bag and wave bye to Harry as Izzy and I start heading out of the cafeteria. As we pass Schellestede, I nudge Izzy with my elbow.

Automatically, she says, "First thing about soccer, Coach always says, is the mental game. It's just as important as the game on the field."

"That's so interesting! Please, tell me more."

As soon as we're in the hall and out of earshot, Izzy stops and turns to me. "I need your help."

Yeah, duh. Why else would she be talking to me? Izzy is the star of the girls' soccer team *and* the coed softball team. Not only does she have a million friends, she has a million admirers, like the sixth grader who looks at Izzy with awe as she scurries past us in the hall.

Izzy notices and gives the girl a nod of recognition, and the girl looks like she might need CPR for her multiple heart attacks.

"In here," I say, and lead Izzy into the girls' room.

We left lunch early, so the bathroom is vacant for now, but in five minutes, a horde of girls will pile in. Izzy follows me into the wheelchair stall, and I shut the door behind us.

"We don't have much time," I say. "What do you need?"

She sighs. "I need to save my clothes."

Okay. This is a new one. I'm not exactly sure

what she means, since Izzy's clothes are, like, two pairs of holey jeans, three busted T-shirts, a pair of raggedy sneakers, and a ball cap. It's not like she's Sophie, who's wearing something new every week.

"Can you be more specific?" I ask.

Izzy takes off her ball cap, tucks her sandy chin-length hair behind her ears, then replaces the hat. "My grandma's coming, and she hates my clothes. My dad makes me dress girly when she visits, so she won't spend the whole time nagging him about how I look, but she usually comes over the summer, so I just go along with it and wear whatever she wants when I'm hanging around the house. But my dad told me last night, she's coming on Saturday for a week, and she said she's gonna throw out all my clothes and buy new stuff while she's here." She looks at me with tears in her eyes. "I can't wear that girly stuff. I can't. I'll do anything not to have to wear a pink dress to school. It's too humiliating."

It's a little ironic that Izzy worries about people

making fun of her for wearing a dress, when people already make fun of her for dressing like a boy. Nobody says anything to her face, because she has a million friends and can kick anybody's butt, but behind her back, some of the snottier dance squad girls call her Izzy-or-Isn't-He.

"Okay, here's what we'll do," I say, thinking out loud. "First step is to save your clothes. Bring your favorite stuff to school every day this week, and I'll keep it safe from your grandma. Then go buy a bunch of junk clothes from Goodwill that you don't care about and stuff your drawers with them. Then your grandma can throw them out. She can even burn them, if she wants."

Izzy shades her eyes, tears rolling down her cheeks. She's red from embarrassment—I don't think anybody at school has ever seen Izzy cry before. But if you're going to cry in front of anybody, it should be me, the human version of the say-no-evil monkey, my paws permanently clasped over my mouth.

"Now we have to find a place for you to store your real clothes and change into them before school. Do you have any friends who live close by you?"

Izzy shakes her head no.

"Friends who live close to school?"

Another no. I frown. You'd think one of Izzy's gazillion friends would live somewhere geographically convenient.

"Maybe . . ." Izzy hesitates, something I imagine she does about as often as she cries. She peeks up at me shyly from behind her hand. "You're on Lincoln Road, right? Could you keep them at your house? And I could come by in the morning to change? It'd only be for five days next week . . ."

"Hmmm." I try not to show my total surprise. This is a much bigger favor than I'm used to doing. And it involves my home life—I like to keep work and home separate. And am I really the most convenient person Izzy could think of for this? Izzy's house isn't even that close to ours. I'd say it's about a twenty-minute walk.

"I can run to your place in five minutes," she says.

Of course she can.

"And I wouldn't have to come back in the afternoon! I could change back into the pink stuff at school, after softball practice, when everyone else goes home, and leave my real clothes here to give you the next day. Please, Glad? Just a week!"

Huh. Now that I'm considering it, it wouldn't be so bad if Izzy came over in the morning, changed in our bathroom, and walked to the bus with me. If she and I became friends, I'd be instantly popular, automatically invited to sit at her lunch table, with the top jocks and beauty queens. I could leave the back corner of the cafeteria and stop scrambling to do favors for everyone. I don't think Dad would mind if Izzy came by in the mornings. And it would shut Mabey up about me not having friends.

Izzy clasps her hands to say "pretty please" and wrinkles her forehead.

"All right," I agree. "I'll do it."

The first few girls have begun to trickle into the

bathroom. I start to exit our stall before we're seen in there together.

"Wait," says Izzy, and I turn to her, surprised. "Do I need to pay you? How does this work? Taye just said you did fixes for people. He didn't say what you charge."

That's because I don't charge anything. I'm looking for something more valuable than money. I'm looking for someone to sit next to me on the bus. An invitation to a party, an offer to hang out after school sometime—that's what I really want. But I don't know how to ask for those things, so I usually wind up settling for the promise of a return favor.

"No charge," I tell Izzy. "But I might ask you for something in the future."

She gives me the grateful look and says the magic words. "Thanks, Glad. I owe you."

Izzy leaves the stall, steps up to the sinks, and starts washing her face with cold water, trying to hide her swollen eyes. I wait a second before leaving the stall, then I brush past her on my way out of the bathroom like we never spoke a word. As much as I want to be seen talking with Izzy, I don't want people to know we were talking about a favor.

Anyway, we'll be talking all the time soon, if everything goes according to plan.

I have a good feeling about this one.

6

Tuesday After School

Agnes and Baxter aren't home when I get there, but Mabey is, as I can tell by the coat and boots by the door. I am starving, so I throw my stuff down in the living room and go to the fridge.

There's only dregs in there: half a lemon, one last splash of milk, and a door full of mostly empty condiment jars with crusty brown gunk around the rims of the lids. That quarter inch of mustard, I realize, has been there since Mom bought it over a year and a half ago.

We really need groceries.

I go up to Mabey's attic, which means climbing a ladder from the second floor and opening a hatch in the ceiling. I'm on the ladder, about to knock on the hatch, but I pause for a second, listening for Mabey's friends.

These days, if I interrupt her when she's got people over, she gets savage. When she used to hang out with Kat and Juliana, her two best friends from grade school, it wasn't a problem for me to come by for two seconds, but now that she has new friends with pierced lips and whatnot, I'm not even allowed to knock.

I hear Mabey talking to someone excitedly, but I don't hear anyone else in her room. She must be on the phone.

"Are you serious?" she asks. "When?" Pause. "That's, like, two weeks from now!"

She's pacing, so her voice goes in and out of earshot. I pick up a few words—"so happy" . . . "how long?" . . . "won't tell them, I promise."

I am trying to stitch these together to get the full story. In, like, two weeks, somebody is going to do something that will make Mabey happy, for an unknown length of time, but it has to be kept secret from some other people.

She paces toward the hatch again, and I overhear her signing off: "Okay. I can't wait. I love you. Bye, Mom."

Mom.

I stand there on the ladder for a second, confused. Mom only calls once a week, always on the home phone, and she only calls in the evenings, when she knows all three of us girls will be here. We can try calling her anytime, but the landline at the farm is constantly busy, and she might not even be there, or she might not have time to talk. I guess Mabey must have called at the exact right time to get through the busy signal. Or she just kept dialing and dialing, the way I used to do.

I wonder if Mabey called Mom or Mom called Mabey. I wonder if this is a special occasion or if Mom and Mabey secretly talk to each other all the time. I did hear Mabey say "I won't tell them, I promise." "Them" must mean me, Agnes, and Dad.

We all know that Mabey is Mom's favorite, but it still hurts to hear that they've been talking in secret. Doesn't Mom want to talk to me, too?

My mind is fully blown, and my body doesn't know where to be. My phone and stuff are in the living room, any food we have is in the kitchen, and I want to flop down on my bed and bury my face in a pillow. I keep turning to go in one direction, then turning around, like a confused tourist. Then I hear Mabey's footsteps coming back toward the hatch.

"Mabes?" I shout.

The hatch opens, and Mabey sticks her head out. Her long brown hair falls straight down, making her look like she's in a horror movie. "What?"

"Um . . ." What was it I had originally come up here to say, before I heard her talking to Mom? Oh, yeah. "We need food."

"Tell Dad," she says.

"He's not home."

She groans like I'm the single most annoying person in the solar system, unless Mars is populated entirely by idiots. "Then text him."

She goes to shut the hatch again. I blurt out, "Were you talking to Mom?"

Her face reappears, and it is scowling. "Were you listening?"

"No, I was about to come up to tell you we have no food. All I heard you say was 'Bye, Mom.'"

Mabey gives me her version of the Lawyer Look, which is the Sullen Stare. I look at her innocently. "Come up," she decides, moving out of the way for me.

I climb the ladder and pull myself through the hatch.

It smells like a hamster cage in Mabey's room. There are dirty clothes and empty mugs and food wrappers on the floor, papers and books and various chargers tossed everywhere. Mabey doesn't seem to mind.

She sits down on her bed, nearly crushing a half-eaten box of powdered doughnut holes, which she passes to me. I sit on her beanbag and start demolishing the doughnut holes one by one.

"Here's the deal," she says. "Mom's coming

home for a visit. You can't tell Dad! And you can't tell Agnes, because she'll tell Dad."

MOM'S COMING HOME.

I gasp, and some donut powder gets sucked into the back of my throat. I start coughing spasmodically. Finally, I get my wheezing under control long enough to ask, "When is she coming? For how long?"

Mabey sighs. "Just a few days, probably around her birthday, but she doesn't have all the details yet. It's like, not everything can be nailed down, the universe is in a constant state of flux . . ."

I count back from her birthday to today. "So three weeks and a day?"

Mabey's eyes perform their automatic roll. "She said 'around then.' You're such a lawyer. You're being so much like Dad."

"I am not."

(And if I am, why is that a bad thing? All I want to know is when Mom's coming, so I know how much time we have to prepare and how long I have

62

to wait. I haven't seen her in over a year and a half. I'm excited, so sue me.)

"Speaking of," Mabey warns me, "you *can't* tell Dad. Or Agnes. That would be the same as telling Dad."

I frown. I'm used to hiding things from Dad, but I don't like hiding things from Agnes, not since the day Mom forgot to pick her up from first grade. Agnes can keep secrets. She's the only person I trust to keep mine. She deserves to know what's happening.

"Okay, but why can't Dad know? I mean, he's going to figure it out when she gets here."

"When she gets her plane ticket, she'll tell Dad. But if something happens and Mom can't make it, she doesn't want him to use it against her, like he always does. Remember when she couldn't come for Thanksgiving? He still mentions that all the time."

Mabey picks up her phone and checks some texts. She is in an awfully good mood. She sure does love being the oldest and bossiest and Mom's favorite. She's going to be a nightmare if she passes her driver's test next month.

"Did you call Mom, or did she call you?" I ask.

Mabey continues to look at her phone and not at me. She absentmindedly twirls her hair with one hand as she speaks. "Why, are you jealous of me and Mom talking?"

Yes. "No."

She raises her head and gives me an "oh really?" eyebrow, then goes back to her texting. "So why does it matter?"

Because if Mom called to talk to Mabey alone, I'll feel left out. But if Mabey called Mom, then I can call Mom, too.

"If you don't like what you hear," Mabey continues smugly, "maybe you shouldn't listen to other people's conversations."

"I wasn't listening to your conversation!"

That came out louder than I meant it to, but I can't help it. I wasn't even trying to eavesdrop, for once! I just wanted something to eat. That's the only reason I came up here. I didn't mean to interrupt Mabey's special phone call with Mom. I didn't ask her to tell me about their super-secret plan. I'm starting to wish I hadn't heard it at all.

Mabey chuckles at my raised voice. "Riiiiiiiight."

Since she's being obnoxious, I think I'll instigate a little. I rise from my seat on the beanbag, wiping a pile of powdered sugar off my lap. "I'm gonna go text Dad," I say.

Mabey takes the bait. "No! I literally just told you not to tell Dad! What is wrong with you?"

"I'm texting him about groceries! God!"

Ha. I leave through the hatch, step down the ladder, and go to my room.

7

Three Hours Later

I'm downstairs in the basement blab-bing to Agnes.

I mean, I have to talk to *somebody*. I'm excited, I'm upset, I'm confused, and talking to Mabey some more isn't going to make me feel better. Agnes deserves to know what's happening, and if I want to fix Dad in time for Mom's visit, I'm going to need her help.

So I wait awhile after dinner, until Mabey hides herself in her attic, and I head down to the basement. Agnes is sitting at her lab table, using a stencil to make labels for some empty mason jars. She's already made labels that say WATER, AMMONIA, and

ECTOPLASM. It is Agnes's dearest wish to become a Ghostbuster.

"I have news." I drop into the busted old recliner Dad dragged down here when he bought a new one for upstairs. "It's about Mom."

"What is it?" Agnes keeps her eyes on her work, guiding her marker carefully down the stencil's edge for a perfectly straight line.

I pause for an imaginary drumroll, then I drop my bomb. "Mom's coming for a visit next month."

Agnes looks up with a happy, hopeful face. "Really? She is? She said so?"

Her reaction makes me smile, too. "Yep. Mabey talked to her earlier, and she said she's coming for her birthday."

Agnes considers this. Her eager expression dims over the "Mabey talked to her" part, but she's still excited. "How long is she coming for?"

"A few days," I guess. Then I admit it. "We're still short on the details."

Agnes's eagerness dims further. "What does Dad say?"

Sigh. Here's the delicate part. "Dad doesn't know yet. And you can't tell him, okay?"

The happy expression is gone. Now she's straight-up frowning. "Why not?"

"Just in case something happens," I say casually. I don't really know what "thing" could happen. I'm just repeating Mabey's words. "You know how Dad gets."

Agnes goes quiet, turning back to her stencil and labels. I watch her squint as she drags her marker around the curve of a C. After a minute: "Is she really going to come, though?"

I draw back, surprised. "Why wouldn't she?"

She shrugs one shoulder, eyes on her work. "Sometimes she says she's going to do something, and then it never happens."

"But you know the Thanksgiving thing wasn't her fault, that was Dad—"

Agnes interrupts me. "It's not just that.

Remember when she kept saying she'd take us to the aquarium, and she never did? She kept promising she'd watch the first episode of *Cosmos* with me, and she never did. And there was that year she was going to make us all handmade Halloween costumes."

Right. Mom didn't make anything until October 30, when Agnes and I started to cry. Then she threw something together at the last minute, scavenging big cardboard boxes from the recycling pile and cutting holes in them for our heads, legs, and arms. "There you go," she said, satisfied. "You're an Amazon delivery."

Technically, those were handmade costumes.

I'm starting to doubt my decision to tell Agnes about Mom's visit. Agnes's skepticism is contagious, and I don't want to catch it. I shift the topic a little. "Anyway, I need your help. We have to fix up Dad before Mom gets here."

She shakes her head no, still concentrating on her work. "I like Dad the way he is."

Argh. Now I understand why Mabey's always rolling her eyes at me. It's not easy to be patient with little sisters. "I just mean the small things. Like the slurping. And the nagging. And the way he always has to be right."

She thinks about this. There's a twitch of her lip as she puts the finishing touches on ETHYL ALCOHOL. As alike as they are, Agnes has her own complaints about Dad. "And how he works too much," she adds finally. "And how he doesn't pay attention sometimes."

"And maybe he could get new clothes or something. And shave the beard." Mom hated the beard Dad grew a few years ago, but he liked the way it looked and wouldn't get rid of it.

Agnes looks at me like I've lost my mind. Had I not been present for the Great Beard Wars of 2017? Can I have forgotten so soon? "Dad won't shave his beard."

"He will if you ask him."

"I don't want him to shave it."

Okay. Deeeeeeeep breath. Agnes is not trying to annoy me on purpose; still, she couldn't do a better job if she tried. "But don't you want Mom to come home?"

"Yes," says Agnes simply.

"So you'll help me fix up Dad?"

Agnes goes silent again. Now she's working on a label that starts with the letters POI. I sincerely hope it's going to say POINTY THINGS when it's finished. "Okay," she finally agrees. "But not the beard, unless we really have to."

Yes! I allow myself a small internal fist pump. With Agnes's superior brain on board, the mission will surely be a success. I know I can get Mabey to join us, too. Agnes and I will work on fixing Dad, and then Mabey will convince Mom to give the new Dad a chance. We'll be an unstoppable team. "Deal."

I rise from my seat and leave Agnes to her work. As many times as I've heard it, it feels so strange to be the one to say it as I start up the basement stairs: "I owe you one."

8

Wednesday Morning

Sophie Nelson needs to return $450 to the student council fund in the next two weeks, or there will be no spring dance.

Oh, and also: Sophie Nelson needs $450.

When Sophie first told me this in the lunchroom on Monday, I thought she was telling an unfunny joke. When I realized she was serious, it got unfunnier.

She must have seen my surprise, because she winced a little and made an "I'm sorry, don't be mad, I'm so cute" face. But honestly, what did she think I could do for her and her cute face? Returning Liz Kotlinski's scarf was one thing; returning almost five hundred dollars that Sophie didn't have was a whole other thing. The amount was too big, the job was impossible, and money is outside my area of expertise.

Sophie was out of luck. Quickly I established that the money was all spent, there was nothing she could return or resell for money, she had no money saved, and there was nobody she could ask for money. So how was I going to help her? If I knew how to get $450, you can bet I'd be sitting here with $450 right now.

But the more Sophie blushed and begged and stressed the importance of bailing out her "friend," the more I started to think, *Hmmm. Maybe.* She would be so grateful, she'd want to be my friend for life, because I had performed this incredible favor. "A favor," Sophie cooed, "that only you could do."

And, I mean, besides wanting Sophie to like me, I knew she was in serious trouble. I couldn't let her—or her invisible "friend"—get caught for stealing that much money. There would definitely be some unpleasant consequences.

So I said, "I'll try."

I am *so* wishing right now that I said no.

Sophie is waiting for me on the steps of the side exit of the gym this morning, as planned. She's in full dance squad mode—they rehearse in the gym a few mornings a week—spangly leotard, ponytail with ribbons, duckface pout. She squeals and claps and air-kisses me when she sees me. We sit down on the steps and get straight to business.

"So are we good?" Sophie eagerly demands.

I'm taken aback. Did Sophie assume I would take care of everything for her, and so quickly? She looks like she expects me to put $450 dollars in her hand right now, then she'll air-kiss me again, tell me she owes me one, and run her spangly butt back to her friends in the gym. Problem solved.

Sophie must have realized this isn't happening, because she furrows her brow in dismay. "I mean, what should we do?"

What should "we" do? What does she mean, "we"? *I* didn't take any money. *I* didn't ask to get dragged into this situation. It's way out of my league—I deal with lost retainers and anonymous chocolates; I don't deal with major theft. I just wish people would realize that the absolute best solution to any problem is to *avoid making the problem in the first place*.

But I did come up with a pretty good plan for her, so I tell her what she needs to do.

"You have to tell the council that you took the money."

Sophie looks at me in horror. I can see her getting ready to remind me that (a) this is the exact, total opposite of what she wants to do and (b) she didn't take it, her "friend" did.

I cut her off.

The strategy I'm suggesting is called Getting There First. Nobody knows that the cash (raised from last week's bake sale, which left everyone in school in a carb coma for the entirety of the afternoon) is missing from the envelope in the locked filing cabinet in the student council HQ, where it's supposed to be, but someone is sure to find out soon. When they do, they'll look at all the people with keys to the cabinet first, and Sophie will be one of the prime suspects. So she needs to buy herself some time.

"Here's what you tell them. You stopped by the council office yesterday after school when nobody was around. You noticed that the file cabinet was unlocked, so you went to check the envelope, and the money was there. And you were *so* relieved that nobody had taken it.

"But it made you nervous that the cabinet was left open, and you wanted to make sure the money was safe. So you put the envelope in your bag, and when your mom picked you up from school, you asked her to take you to the bank. The money is safe in the bank, and you can get it in two weeks, when it's needed. You got it?"

Sophie nods, speechless.

"Step one, cover up the problem. Then you can move on to step two—getting the money."

Sophie's vocal cords rally for a second, then quit again. "You . . . that . . ." She shakes her head as though she's trying to wake herself from a dream. "Whoa."

I don't know if this is a good *whoa* or a bad *whoa*, until she takes my hand and presses it between hers like she's about to ask me to marry her. Her face breaks into a huge, lip-glossy smile.

"You. Are. A genius." She is still a little mind-blown, and she is squeezing my hand hard enough to liquefy it, but she manages a few more words. "That's . . . that's, like, the *perfect* story."

I feel myself blushing with pride. This is why I do what I do: the gratitude, and the compliments, and the satisfaction of a job well done. I can already see myself sitting next to Sophie in free study or getting picked for her team in gym. I'm going to need some new clothes. "Well, I'm not a *genius* . . ."

Sophie lets go of my hand, thank God, and

shakes her head slowly in disbelief. Her eyes are so wide, it looks like she just saw Bigfoot. "No, you are. Everybody knows it, too. Everyone says, 'Glad can get you out of anything,' and they're right! You are a genius liar. You're like the Einstein of lies."

Ouch.

I know Sophie means this as a compliment, but words like *liar* and *lies* offend me. I don't tell *lies*. I tell *stories*. And, as far as I know, the stories are true. I mean, I don't know what Sophie was doing yesterday after school—maybe she stopped by the student council office, saw the cash in the unlocked cabinet, and took it to the bank. And if she didn't, well, I'm not the one who's going to the council to tell them that story. It's a story when I come up with it. It only becomes a lie when she says it.

I'm not a liar. I'm a *helper*.

"Not lies," I correct her. "Excuses, alibis, and cover stories, but never lies."

"Right," says Sophie. "Whatever. I could, like, kiss you right now. I can't wait to hear step two."

Fortunately, she's not serious about the kissing, because I am saving my first kiss for a day when the thought of kissing someone outside my family doesn't nauseate me. "You'll hear step two," I say. "After you do step one."

(Also, after I figure out what step two is going to be.)

Sophie jumps to her feet and claps, as if the dance squad has spilled out from the gym onto the steps. "Okay, well. I better get back inside. You're amazing, Glad! Thanks!"

And that's it. She bounces through the door and it swings shut behind her. I hear her laughing and clapping and rejoining her squad. One loose spangle glitters at me from where she sat two seconds ago.

I am amazing. I am a genius. Everybody says so. I am the best.

I am also—as usual—alone.

9

Wednesday
Fifth Period

I'm at my desk in the back row, taking notes on the important history lessons of the day.

TREATY OF GHENT

- Ended War of 1812
- War was between US and UK/Ireland
- But treaty was signed in Belgium?
- Canada was also somehow involved?
- Unclear, also, boring

TREATY OF SAM BOYD AND EVELYN FERSZT

Dear Evelyn,

I'm sorry Ms. Mundaca gave you detention for looking at my test on Monday. I should have pushed my paper closer to you so you didn't have to lean over so far to see it. Next time I promise to make it easier for you to see. Remember, if you kill me, you'll have to look at Jackson's answers instead of mine, and Jackson sucks at math. So please accept my apologies. Also, you are very beautiful.
Sam

MADISON'S DAILY REVERSE-
CATFISHING TEXTS

> madison plz dont be mad cuz i cant visit at spring break like i promised 🥲☹️
> i wish i cld but u know my medical condition means i cant fly 😊🙃
> ILY so much ♡ ♡ ♡ ♡ ♡ ♡

WHAT I WISH I COULD SAY TO TAYE

Taye. Dude. If you want a response to your gifts, YOU HAVE TO SAY THE GIFTS ARE FROM YOU. This should BE A LOT MORE OBVIOUS TO YOU.

OPERATION MOM

Visit Preparation
- Plan fun things:
    Pottery studio
    Feed ducks at park
    Karaoke
- Reservations at fancy restaurant?
- Get food she likes—IMPORTANT: must be organic
- CLEAN UP and make house look nice.
- Fresh flowers
- 1980s music
- Mood lighting
- Slippers and robe in case she forgets hers
- AVOID letting her do housework. treat her like a guest.
- Make sure she doesn't even touch a dirty dish.

Hide Upcoming Visit from Dad

- Use code words.
- Meet in attic or basement.
- When it's time to tell him, have Agnes do it.

Fix Up Dad

- Clothes
- Beard
- Personality
- Tone of voice/tiny smile
- Slurping!
- Have Agnes save up good grades, tell Dad about them right before Mom comes.
- Have Mabey be nice to Dad.
- All of us stay out of trouble.

Things to Say to Mom About Dad

- "Dad's really lightened up a lot lately. He lets me watch PG-13 movies now, even though I'm still twelve."
- "Dad was saying how much he misses your singing around the house."

- "Last time Dad talked to Grandma June, he said she was being too critical and picky and that every time you and Grandma June argued, you were right."

Things to Say to Dad About Mom
- "We miss her."
- "Be nice to her."
- "Get her to want to come home."

10

Wednesday Afternoon

Agnes and Baxter are midway through a game of chess when I get home.

I put my stuff down in the hall and join them in the kitchen. They both greet me without looking up from the board on the table.

"Hey, Glad the Impaler."

I'll give this much to Baxter: He occasionally comes up with something I haven't heard before. Also, he brought bread and cheese and butter, which are spread out on the counter next to a dirty pan and a crumby plate—hello, grilled cheese sandwiches.

I go over to the counter and start fixing myself one or two. (Two.)

"What's up, Botox?"

"Getting massacred in chess." He moves his knight, which temporarily disappears in his absurdly large hand.

Agnes moves a pawn and picks up his knight. "He's letting me win."

Baxter looks up at me, mouthing, *I'm not letting her win.*

I fry my sandwiches until they're gooey, put them on the crumby plate, and sit down to let them cool. Watching Baxter and Agnes play chess is boring. I have some homework to do, but I don't feel like doing it yet.

"Where's Mabes?"

"In her room," says Agnes. "With Lip Ring and Hyena Laugh."

She means Mabey's friends Sybil and Nomi. (Whose name, BTW, is really Naomi—she dropped the *a* right around the time Sybil got her lip ring. Like, "You're going to pierce your lip? Well, I'm going to pierce *my name*.")

A brief wistful look passes over Baxter's face. Sometimes I forget that Baxter is still in college, because he dresses like he's seventy-three, and he wears his hair cut super-short. He's what Mom would call "a normal"—an ordinary, boring guy who plays by all the rules. I don't think he's ever hung out in an attic with someone called Lip Ring.

"Checkmate." Agnes moves her rook and takes Baxter's queen. "Good game. Want to play again?"

Baxter sighs and starts setting up his pieces for another slaughter. I see an opportunity to interrupt here to get some advice. Dad always tells us, *When you don't know what to do, ask an adult.* Baxter qualifies.

"Wait," I say. "Question for you. If you were in middle school and you needed to make money quickly, what would you do?"

"E-mail scam," Agnes answers immediately. Baxter and I raise our eyebrows at each other. She should have needed a second to think about the question before going straight to fraud. Agnes looks up from resetting the chessboard. "What? This is hypothetical, right?"

"No, serious question. But not for me. Asking for a friend."

OMG, I realize. *That's Sophie's line. And I'm saying it about her!*

"Get an after-school job," Baxter suggests. "Mow lawns, do yard work, walk dogs, babysit . . ."

"Mmmmm . . ."

I already got this advice from Google. It's hard to imagine Sophie picking up dog poop, and she'd need a lot of dog poop to get to $450. "What about something that actually pays?"

"E-mail scam," Agnes repeats quietly. She pushes a pawn forward to start a new game.

"Well, if it was me," says Baxter, ignoring the pawn, "I would sell my expertise. Like your dad does. People pay him a certain amount of money per hour because he's an expert at tax law. What are you an expert at? What can you do for people that they can't do for themselves? Or what skills can you teach? What's something you know how to do that other people would pay to learn?"

Huh. What is Sophie an expert at? Air-kissing? Dance-squadding? I don't think she can sell air-kissing lessons. Air-kissing is pretty self-explanatory. She's good with makeup and hair and clothes, but there're a million makeup and hair tutorials online for free. Something with clothes, maybe . . .

I hear Mabey and her friends coming down the stairs. Mabey marches into the kitchen, and Lip Ring and Hyena Laugh linger in the hall, absorbed in their phones.

"You guys want grilled cheese?" Mabey calls to them, ignoring me and Agnes and Baxter. Some vague syllables emit from the girls in the hall. Mabey flings open the fridge and frowns at the contents. "There's no food in this house."

Baxter looks up from the chessboard. "Good afternoon, Mabel," he says pleasantly. "How are you today?"

Mabey doesn't even bother to reply. "We need

food," she says, slamming the fridge door. She rejoins her friends and they stomp back upstairs.

"Rude," mutters Agnes.

"Seriously," I agree.

The man brought grillable cheese into the house. He deserves our respect.

Baxter looks more amused than upset. "Don't worry about it." He takes a bishop from Agnes. "It's always a joy to see your sister, whatever her mood."

I assume he's being sarcastic, but I can't always tell with Baxter. He could be sincere. He's sincere about a lot of crazy stuff. One time he said to me, "You haven't lived until you've tasted raw sea urchin," and I thought he was kidding, until he revealed a take-out container with *raw sea urchin* inside. So you never know.

I put my dishes in the dishwasher and go upstairs to my room, leaving Baxter and Agnes to their game. Searching online for "sell expertise" gets me a bunch of articles from business magazines about "leveraging your position" and "best biz dev practices." I'm trying to translate these into English, but it's no use, so I give up on the Sophie plan for now.

I take out some reading for school and lie there on my bed until Dad comes home and yells at us from the hallway.

"Girls! Dinner! We're having grilled cheese!"

11

Thursday Morning

Izzy just punched me on the bus.

It's good, though. She meant it in a good way. She got on the bus at her stop, the one after mine, and as she passed my seat, she socked me in the bicep and said, "What's up, jackweed."

"Ow." I shifted away and rubbed my arm. "What's up."

Izzy swaggered toward the back to sit with her sports friends. "What's up, you jackweeds," she said, punching Taye and Jackson, who obligingly punched her back.

"Shut up, jackweed."

"Shut up, dairy fairy."

It took most of the twenty-minute bus ride for the pain to subside, and for me to realize: To Izzy, punching someone and calling them a jackweed is a sign of friendship. Izzy and I have our private business relationship, of course—yesterday, she passed me three T-shirts, two sweatshirts, and a pair of sneakers that smell like rotting roadkill. But for her to punch me like that? That's not business. That's personal.

So now I feel pretty good.

I'm making my way through the various cliques standing around in front of school when I see the flannel-clad blur of Jasmine the drummer in my peripheral vision, hurrying my way. She catches up to me, grabs me by my sore arm, and drags me a few feet away from the crowd.

"Hey," she says. She's out of breath and her face is flushed. "I need another excuse for missing band."

"Another excuse? So soon?" I frown. This is pushing it, in my professional opinion. Gerber may have swallowed the "auditioning for a band" story

I gave her on Monday, but Jasmine shouldn't try to cram another story down his throat until he's had time to digest the first one. "You can't keep skipping band and needing excuses."

Jasmine's surprise shows on her face. She's not used to hearing me say no—nobody is. "I know. I won't, I swear, just help me out, please."

I don't like this. I don't like how intense she's being, how nervous she seems. This is not the Jasmine who sits in class tapping her foot methodically to the beat of an internal song. This isn't the girl who sprained her ankle while playing softball and proudly took a million pictures of her gnarly foot as it was getting bandaged. Now she's cringing and gnawing at her fingernails (what's left of them).

"Please," she begs. "Last one. Please, Glad."

Yeah, something's not right here. Problem is, I'm too good at what I do. The answer has already formed in my head, and it wants to come out of my mouth. Jasmine looks at me with desperation, and I give in.

"Okay. Your garage band audition went so well, you got a second audition. That's why you missed practice."

Jasmine lets out the breath she's been holding. "Oh my God, Glad, that's perfect. Thank you so, so much. I owe you one."

She turns and skitters away.

I have taken maybe three whole steps toward the door, when I hear, "Pssst! Glad!" Madison Graham is urgently beckoning me from a nearby bush.

Ugh. Didn't I just send some "James" texts to Madison yesterday? It feels like I keep dealing with the same problems for the same people. I'm starting to think getting punched by Izzy is the best thing that's going to happen to me today.

"Hey." Madison darts out from her hiding place and pulls me behind the shrubbery. "I need more texts."

Okay, what is going on this morning? Why are people coming up to me and asking for follow-up favors? I am not *soda*. There are no *free refills*. And why does everyone want to push their luck? Is today National Terrible Idea Day?

"Madison, this has been going on for weeks now." I try to say this gently but firmly. This was supposed to be a one- or two-time thing, not an ongoing three-week job, and I'm a little sick of texting love notes to Madison Graham all the time when I barely even like her. "I really think you should let this go."

Madison looks as confused as Jasmine did. I'm not supposed to turn down requests; that's not how it's supposed to work with me. People are supposed to come to me for favors, and I'm supposed to shut up and do them.

"Please, Glad. I can't stop getting texts."

I sympathize, I really do. I understand how embarrassed she'd be if her friends found out she was using a fake boyfriend to make them jealous.

"But this is just going to go on and on," I explain. "You can't keep this up forever." More important, *I* can't keep this up forever. "Why don't you 'break up' with James?"

Madison is shocked by the suggestion. "But . . . but I love him."

Her voice, when she says *I love him,* is 100 percent sincere. And that is 1,000 percent insane. I might need to take her by the shoulders and slap her a few times to bring her back to reality: *You do realize that I am James, right? You do remember that you're here outside of school, talking to me, Gladys Burke, so that I will text you from my phone number, which you have saved under the name James, right? I know that I am very good at pretending to be somebody else, but we're both clear that there is no real person named James who lives in Canada and is your boyfriend, are we not?*

From our secluded spot, I see Madison's friends standing by their usual bench, looking around to see where she might be. It's almost time to go inside.

"Please," she begs. "I'll do whatever you want."

"Okay, okay, fine." I just want to get her away from me. "He'll text you by lunchtime, okay?"

"Phew," she says, finally calming down. She even manages to smile. "You scared me for a second there."

And you scared me for a full five minutes, Madison. In fact, you're still scaring me.

Madison walks away from our shrub and I linger for a second to collect myself. This day is already crazy, and school hasn't even begun.

"Gladys!"

"Ahh!"

I jump about eight feet in the air. If I was holding a hot beverage, I would be showered in it right now. I twirl around in a panic to see who startled me. Of course, it's Schellestede.

And wow! Who knew my heart could beat this fast? My whole body says *run*, but I'm caught, unable to look away as Schellestede narrows her eyes at me. Amazingly, her narrow-eyed stare is even stronger and more concentrated than her overpowering normal-eyed stare. Soon my brain will turn to slush and start leaking from my ears.

"Is there a reason you're holding a conference with Ms. Graham behind a bush?"

"Uh . . ."

So many reasons spring to mind. *Madison split her pants and needed a safety pin. Madison and I are working on a botany project involving local shrubbery. Madison and I are secretly in love, and you just interrupted our tender moment, you crackly old witch.*

"No," I say meekly.

Schellestede breaks into her chilling smile. "Then you might want to go inside right now and begin the school day."

By golly, she's right! I have never wanted anything as much as I want to go inside right now and begin the school day. I scoot away from Schellestede and dash through the doors like they're giving out free unicorns in first period. School. Yes. Perfect. Ideal.

Note: When the idea of being in class starts to sound appealing, it's time to rethink your life choices.

12

Thursday Lunch

Harry Homework isn't looking so hot.

I noticed it earlier in science, when he said nothing, not even to himself. Harry learned long ago not to answer every question just because he could, but usually he mutters the answers under his breath. Today he sat in silence, resting his forehead on his desk, staring straight into his lap.

Now he's sitting at our table in the lunchroom with his face in his hands. I slide in next to him with my greasy bag of leftover grilled cheese, and he doesn't look up.

"What's up?" I ask.

"Not much," he says into his hands. "I'll just be dead soon. No big deal."

"What happened?"

Harry lifts his head and looks at me with a woozy expression. "Schellestede called my parents in for a conference yesterday and told them I'm close to getting suspended. I told her, 'All these study guides are in a million places online! It's not against the rules to share them!' But now she's saying I'm not allowed to give any student any kind of study aid." He looks up at me, plaintive. "She shut me down, Glad. I'm through. The eighth graders are going to kill me."

My mind automatically starts working on Harry's problem. Who is the largest person who currently owes me a favor? It's about time I cashed in a few of those. Is there any way for Harry to get from the bus to the classroom and vice versa without walking through the throng of students? Can somebody distract Schellestede for the next three months of school? Not likely, as I am reminded, watching her from across the room. She's not even looking directly at us, and I can still feel the suffocating weight of her stare.

"Did you tell your parents why you do it?" I ask.

Harry looks at me like I'm crazy. His parents are so overprotective, Harry barely gets sunlight. If they hovered over him any more, they'd be umbrellas.

"Do you know what my parents would do if they thought I was being bullied?" Harry ticks off the list on his fingers. "They would file a lawsuit against the school district. They would sue the other parents. They'd write letters to the news-papers. They'd start petitions online. They'd try to get on the local news. And knowing them? They'd send me to school with a paid escort."

I almost choke on my sandwich. A paid escort? Lord, have mercy.

Where is André the Anti-Bullying Aardvark when you need him? Why can't he hold an assem-bly for parents and tell them how *not* to deal with bullying? Adults never seem to get it: They live in Adult World, and kids live in Kid World, and those are two separate planets. Here on Kid World, going to an adult about bullying is like going to a

Laundromat about groceries. You're probably not going to get what you want.

"So what do you do now?" I ask.

He smiles ruefully. "I was just about to ask you that."

"Could you tell your parents you're not being challenged here? Like, Elmhaven isn't providing the right 'learning environment' for you? Maybe your folks would switch you to a new school."

Harry nixes this. "Believe me, I've thought about switching schools. My parents and I toured this special private school last year. It looked great at first, but the minute I went to the bathroom, I saw some older kid picking on a kid like me." He shakes his head at the memory. "Wherever I go, there's going to be bullies."

"But at least you could start over. You could get back into the homework game. And there'd be no Schellestede to shut you down, so—"

Harry interrupts, his face flushed with frustration. "You don't get it. Nothing would be different at a new school. This is always going to happen to me, because this is who I am. I'm the little brainiac who gets picked on. I can't change being smart. I can't get bigger overnight. There are always going to be bullies. I am always going to have this problem."

I have no answer for this.

Society has no answer for this.

The whole human race has no answer for this.

"It's not worth switching schools," Harry concludes. "At least I have some friends here."

He means me, I realize. Me and a hyperverbal sixth grader named Forrest and Leila Marshan, who is such a Goody Two-Shoes, she is on the verge of sprouting another foot so she can level up to Goody Three. I don't know if there's any way for Forrest or Leila to help Harry, but I will do everything I can for him.

Harry and I finish lunch relatively undisturbed. Taye tries to get my attention with a discreet wave, but I jerk my head in Schellestede's direction and shake my head, so he stays away. When we're done eating and I go to toss my garbage, Sophie gets up from her table to do the same, and our vectors converge at the trash can.

"Hey," she whispers, in case I thought this was an accidental meeting.

"What's up," I murmur.

Sophie is bubbling with barely contained glee. "Step one went great. They loved the bank story. But we're less than two weeks away from the dance. What's step two?"

Step two is still under development, but it's shaping up. I lean forward and whisper to Sophie: "We're going to sell your expertise."

13

Thursday Night

I'm sitting on my bed, listening to a busy signal.

I've been trying to call the phone at the farm for about ten minutes already, hanging up and redialing over and over. No luck so far. It's frustrating, but it's given me some time to rehearse what I want to say.

Hi, Mom! When are you coming to visit? No, that sounds too pushy, and Mom hates to be pushed. *Hi, Mom! Mabey says you're coming to visit!* No. I shouldn't bring up the visit right away. I should ask about the farm first. *Hi, Mom! How are the baby chickens doing?* That sounds better, but I don't want to talk about the chickens.

Hi, Mom. I miss you. Please come home for good. I promise I'll make Dad change. Just come home and be our mom again.

I hang up and redial, and this time the call goes through. A man answers immediately. "Hello?"

"Um, hi." I was unprepared for someone to actually answer. Now that I got through, I'm nervous. "Is Suzanne there, please?"

"Don't know, but I can check for you. Who's calling?"

I feel shy, embarrassed to be taking up this man's time and tying up the phone. "Her daughter."

"Hang on, I'll see if she's around."

I hear him put the phone down, then I wait in silence for a minute. I wonder if this phone call was a good idea. What if Mom's busy and I'm interrupting her? What if she's mad that I called? I should just hang up.

"Mabes?" Mom gets on the phone sounding rushed.

This was a bad idea.

"No, it's Glad."

I'm so afraid she'll be disappointed that it's me instead of Mabey, but she sounds delighted. "Bun-Bun! Gladiola! My brave and beautiful Gladiator!" Then her voice gets serious. "Why are you calling? Is everything okay?"

"Yeah, I just wanted to find out . . . I just wanted to talk to you."

"Oh, great!" She sounds relieved. "Listen, now's not a great time, I only have a minute before I need to go, but tell me what's going on. How are you?"

"Good." There's so much to tell her since the last time we talked. *Mom, I'm making friends with two of the most popular girls at school. Izzy's on the softball and soccer teams, and Sophie's on the dance squad, and I'm helping them both with their problems. And I'm going to fix up Dad so you'll love him again.* "Mabey says you're coming to visit."

I hear displeasure in Mom's voice. "She wasn't supposed to say anything until it's final."

"Don't worry, I won't tell Dad." I'm proud to say

I've never told Dad anything Mom didn't want him to know. "But . . . you are coming, right?"

"Yes," she declares, after a short pause. "I'm booking a flight next week. I'll let your father know as soon as I have the reservation." Another pause. "He and I . . . We need to talk in person, so we can work some things out."

I burst out cheering. "Yay! Mom! I can't wait to see you!"

"Listen," she says. "I have to go. I'm so sorry I can't talk more right now, but I promise I'll call soon and let you know when I'm coming. I can't wait to see you, BunBun. Love you!" She makes a kissing sound and ends the call.

I hang up, part happy and part unsatisfied. I never get to talk to Mom enough. Just long enough to remind me how much I miss her. Even during our weekly calls, Agnes and Mabey are always waiting for their turn to talk to her, and sometimes Dad is hovering, too, waiting for us to wrap it up so they can have a quick, curt chat about . . . finances, or whatever. I'm not sure what they talk about—he shoos us out of the room and keeps his voice low most of the time, unless he's yelling "That's not what I said!" or "Don't hang up on—damn it!"

But when Mom comes home, we'll have time to talk. She won't be feeding chickens or building kilns, so she won't have to rush off anywhere. Agnes and Mabey won't be impatiently waiting. Mom will be right here next to me, where I can see her and feel her.

And if I do my job right, she'll want to stay.

14

Friday First Period

I'm sitting in math class, trying to understand various variables.

$$X = 2+Y/5$$

- If y is 3, solve for x.
- You know what, I'm getting kind of tired of solving for x.
- Why doesn't x solve for itself for a change?

**IDEA FOR SOMEBODY WHO NEEDS
TO SOLVE THINGS FOR HERSELF**

<u>Sophie Nelson Fashion Consulting for Parents</u>

Are you a busy parent with no time to shop for clothes?

Do your kids nag you about how you dress?

Are you thinking it might be time to update your look?

Sophie can help!

Fashion expert Sophie Nelson is now offering her

services as a wardrobe consultant, personal shopper, and

stylist for parents who want to renew their image.

Reasonable rates!

Contact Sophie for details and availability.

Sophie Nelson Fashion Consulting for Parents

"We help parents be less embarrassing."

FINAL BREAK-UP TEXTS TO MADISON

> Madison i have had some terrible health news. the
  worst possible

> To spare u i am breaking up with u now

> 💔 i will always love u but u will never hear from
  me again

> Farewell my love...

WHAT I WISH I COULD SAY TO BECKY LEWIS

Rebecca, I have given your problem careful consideration. I'm sorry to say I don't know how to solve it. Nobody is going to call you Rebba. It's not going to happen. I suggest you shoot for Becca.

PROJECT HARRY

Adversaries

- Russell Sharpe and his eighth-grade goons

   Strengths: Strength. Also: height, weight, numbers, meanness

   Weaknesses: Easily confused, usually in trouble

   Strategies: Avoid. If possible, deploy Schellestede.

- Eighth-grade burnouts

   Strengths: Don't care about anything

   Weaknesses: Slow moving, usually hungry, lose focus easily

   Strategies: "What's that over there?" Bribe with snacks.

- Overenthusiastic jocks
    Strengths: Strength, boisterousness, desire to be punching people at all times
    Weaknesses: Not actually evil, just bored
    Strategies: Duck
- Random jerks
    Strengths: Victims never know who they are or when they're coming, element of surprise.
    Weaknesses: ?
    Strategies: ?

<u>Vulnerable Times</u>
- Before school. (Solution: Enter school early for some club or activity, e.g., dance squad?)
- Between classes. (Some kind of escort/bodyguard? Who?)
- Lunch. (Move to new table with more people? Closer to door?)
- Gym. (Wear gym clothes under regular clothes to

avoid locker room, try not to sweat too much, after class put on regular clothes over gym clothes.)
- After school (?)

<u>Self-Defense</u>
- Whistle/alarm
- Bug spray (like Mace, but less illegal).
- Develop halitosis?

<u>Possible Allies</u>
Taye—Ask him to keep jocks from roughhousing.
Izzy—Not sure what for but could definitely be useful.
Biggest bully in our class…Evelyn Ferszt?

15

Friday Lunch

I'm going toward our table to discuss my notes on Harry's case with him, when Sophie calls my name.

"Glad! Hey!"

She beckons me over to where she's sitting with a mix of A+ people from the dance squad and the student council. Why is she waving at me to come over there? I don't belong there. I belong over in the corner, with Harry and his sardines, and I'm about to just wave back to Sophie and then go join him there, but she calls me again.

"Glad!" she insists, waving me over.

Okay, I'm not about to ignore an invite from

Sophie Nelson. But seriously, what is she doing? I doubt she wants to discuss her private business with me in front of her friends, so maybe she's trying to help me socially? I appreciate it, but I'd rather not start my socializing career with the whole dance squad at once. The Elmhaven dance squad is ranked seventeenth in our state for dance, but they are the number one world champions of being shady. I don't even know how Carolina Figgis can see straight anymore, because she's always looking sideways at people.

I walk over to the A+ table and stand nearby. "Hey."

Carolina Figgis looks like she's smelling a dirty sock. Carolina's backup duo, Desiree Adamo and Hannah Conley, raise their eyebrows and smirk at each other. Sophie hops up from her seat, air-kisses me, clasps my arm, and pulls me into an empty chair.

"You guys, Glad wants to join the decorating committee for the dance, isn't that awesome?"

Uh, who wants to do what now? I don't want to decorate for the dance. I don't even want to dance for the dance. But what is my dignity, next to Sophie's privacy? Sophie needs an excuse to be friends with me, so I try to smile like someone who enjoys decorating things.

"Awesome," says Hannah, her voice thick with sarcasm.

Hannah, please don't make me remind you of that thing I did for you that time. Queen Carolina would be furious if she knew you were the one who wrote that stuff about her on the bathroom wall.

Sophie ignores Hannah and turns to me. "We're just starting the meeting, so you didn't miss anything. Rich, what were you saying?"

"We need to agree on a smell that represents spring," says student council president Rich Savoy. "The scent-scape is a vital part of the décor. The day after the dance, nobody's gonna remember what was on the walls. But a *smell* lasts in your memory for years."

Desiree disagrees. "Everybody's gonna remember what was on the walls, because it's in all the pictures. You can't take a picture of a smell."

I look across the lunchroom at Harry, alone at our table and vulnerable. He looks up from his phone and sees me at Sophie's side. I give him a little wave, but he doesn't return it. I notice that Schellestede's not at her regular post. Wherever she is, I hope she's watching Harry as closely as she did when she was trying to bust up his homework business.

"I don't care," Hannah drawls. "As long as we don't do pastels. Pastels are so done."

Carolina Figgis sits on Sophie's other side, shooting dagger looks at me. Carolina and Sophie have been best friends since they were nine; they never even went through that phase where they made other friends and dropped each other. And yet Queen Carolina—glamorous, popular, enviable Carolina—seems to think I'm some kind of threat to their friendship. She stares at me, perplexed and annoyed, like, *What are* you *doing here?*

I'm not sure what I'm doing here. I mean, I know we're here to talk about buying stuff and throwing it around the gym, but I have nothing to say on that matter. And yet the longer I sit listening to people debate balloons versus no balloons, the more I start getting into it. The topic shifts to lighting, and I suggest, "What about Christmas lights wrapped around the tables? We wouldn't even have to buy them, if people could bring them from home."

President Rich looks pleased. "Did everybody catch that? What do you think about bringing Christmas lights from home? I think it's a great idea. And cost-effective."

"With foil tablecloths?" asks Sophie excitedly. "In spring colors? That would look amazing."

So there, Carolina. I'll tell you what I'm doing here: sitting with my friend Sophie Nelson. Meeting with the decorating committee. Acting like a regular person with regular hobbies. Eating my lunch. Not fixing anything.

That's when Madison shows up.

Heads turn as she rushes through the cafeteria, her face red and her expression distraught. She's going for my usual table, but then she catches sight of me at Sophie's side and changes direction.

Madison *freakin'* Graham. Just when I'm hanging out at the A+ table, she's got to barge in and make a scene. I stand up to head her off, and she gets right up in my face. "I need to talk to you," she growls.

Everybody around us is giddy with excitement watching this go down.

"Ooh, lovers' spat," murmurs Hannah, and Carolina laughs.

It is decided: I am going to kill Madison.

"Hallway," I say as calmly as I can.

The *ooh* noise rises from the tables like helium as forty-five pairs of eyeballs follow us out the door.

In the hall, Madison whirls around to face me. "You *murderer*," she spits.

Huh? Is Madison psychic? Did she just hear me decide to kill her? "What?"

This just makes her madder. "Don't try to act innocent! You killed him!"

Okay, I literally have no idea . . . Wait a minute. Oh my God. I *do* have an idea what she's talking about. She's talking about the texts she got this morning from "James."

I put my hands up, innocent, and try to speak calmly. "Madison, I didn't kill anybody. James is not a real person."

She doesn't even hear this. She comes toward me and I bring my hands into a defensive position.

"I would have done anything you asked," she hisses. "But you had to take him away from me."

In her eyes, I see the glassy stare of a maniac. How can *nobody* be nearby right now? Doesn't *anybody* need a favor? Where's Jasmine, trying to grub another excuse? Where's Schellestede, trying to catch me in the act? Because HELLO, I'M IN THE ACT OUT HERE, COME CATCH ME IN IT, PLEASE.

I raise my voice. "Madison. Calm down. You are taking this way too seriously . . ."

The maniac isn't listening. She smiles, showing

me her shiny teeth. "No, Glad. You took him from me, and I'm going to take something from you."

Take something from me? This is *insane*. You know, I used to whine because Dad's and Agnes's allergies meant we couldn't ever get a cat or a dog, but right now I'm sincerely grateful that we never got a pet, because I would be fearing for its life.

"What are you talking about?" I ask nervously.

Madison leans back on her heels, a satisfied look on her face. "You'll find out."

Yeah. I'd rather not find out. I'd rather not even think about it. I'm getting images of my beloved stuffed bunny, Otis, with a noose around his neck and little *X*s for eyes. I start backpedaling in my calmest voice. "Okay, Madison, hang on. James isn't dead yet. He's very sick, but he's still alive. So why don't we both relax, and we can talk about this again on Monday . . ."

Her expression instantly changes, and hope blooms in her eyes. "You'll bring him back? Seriously? Oh, Glad, thank you, thank you, thank you!"

Just like that, I'm her friend again. Two seconds

ago, she was threatening me with some unspecified revenge, and now she's—*oof*—hugging me. Still, when she breaks away and looks into my eyes, I see a little bit of the maniac lingering in her stare.

"You promise you'll bring him back?" she demands.

No. I don't want to bring "him" back. This has officially become way too freaky for me. Madison needs to take a break from her fantasy life and rejoin the rest of us in the bone-crushing world of reality. I don't want to make a promise I know I'm going to break—no lies, that's one of my rules. Excuses, alibis, and cover stories, but never outright lies.

But sometimes, I have to break my own rule.

"I promise," I assure Madison. "I'll bring James back."

16

Friday Afternoon

Agnes and Mabey and I are plotting in the attic.

Mabey is sitting cross-legged on her bed amid a riot of books, papers, and clothes. I'm in the beanbag chair, and Agnes is sitting on the floor, playing with the little round magnets she got at the hardware store. I'm telling them about the talk I had with Mom.

"Anyway, she said she's definitely coming, and she'll know exactly when by next week."

Mabey folds her arms across her chest and rolls her eyes at me. "That's the same thing she told me. We already knew that." She's annoyed that I got to speak to Mom apart from our weekly group call. I know the feeling.

I refer to my phone, which displays my Operation Mom notes. "We don't have time to argue, okay? We have a lot of work to do before she gets here."

Agnes isn't saying much. She keeps trying to push the reverse sides of two magnets together, and they keep resisting. I'm about to read my notes aloud when she asks quietly, "Does Dad even want Mom to come home?"

Mabey answers slowly and exaggeratedly, like Agnes is a three-year-old. "Of course Dad wants Mom to come home. Dad didn't want to get separated from Mom in the first place. She's the one who left."

"I know," Agnes says. One of the magnets flips and joins the other. She pries them apart again. "But I think he's too mad at her now."

Mabey looks at me, like, *I TOLD you we shouldn't tell her.* I jump in before Agnes can ask another question.

"Anyway, we have to start fixing Dad *now*, which means new clothes. My friend Sophie's going to help with a new look. She's a fashion expert."

Yes, it's time for the test launch of Sophie Nelson Fashion Consulting for Parents. After school today, I slipped her the notes I made this morning, and she texted me ten seconds later with a fiesta of overjoyed emojis.

Agnes likes my idea, but Mabey brushes it off. "Okay, but that's just his clothes. What are we going to do about his personality?"

I'm already on it. "I was thinking we could trade him—for every annoying habit he gives up, we could give up one of ours. Like, Mabey, if he quits slurping, you could quit muttering. Agnes, if he quits nagging, you could quit setting off the smoke alarms."

"That only happened twice!" Agnes protests. "And I didn't set fire to anything. I was trying to get one off the wall to take it apart."

Mabey turns to me. "What are you going to quit?"

Good question. What do I do that annoys Dad? I could stop flipping water bottles, since I'll never get the hang of it anyway. I could stop belching super-loud in public. I could stop leaving dishes in the sink.

"You could quit snooping," Mabey says pointedly. "That might be nice for everyone."

"You could quit interrupting," suggests Agnes.

"You could quit eavesdropping," adds Mabey.

All right, I get the point, I have annoying habits. They can stop listing them now. But Agnes has one more: "You could quit trying to fix everything."

"Ooh, good one," says Mabey.

LOL. Additional LOL. *O* sandwich on *L* bread. I *know* Agnes and Mabey don't want me to stop fixing things. Who would make a plan to fix up Dad, if it weren't for me? Who would arrange it so Mabey could sneak out after midnight on Halloween to TP houses with her friends? Who would help Agnes convince Dad she wasn't using the clothes dryer as a centrifuge?

"We can talk about that later," I decide. "But we agree on the principle, right? We quit stuff Dad hates and Dad quits stuff we hate?"

Agnes and Mabey nod in agreement. We are all in.

The meeting breaks up, Agnes goes downstairs to her lab, and I go to our room to do some reading for school. I sit on my bed and open a book and look at the words inside. But I'm not reading—I'm thinking about Agnes's magnets, how she tried pressing the wrong sides together, and how the squishy tension between them always forced them apart. How she kept trying, like if she pushed them hard enough, she could overcome the scientific fact:

You can't join polar opposites.

17

Saturday

Dad and I are wandering around the auditorium at Agnes's elementary school while she sets up for the science fair.

All around us, third and fourth graders are assembling their hilariously slanted handwritten signs, their lumpy papier-mâché solar systems, and their totally basic, not-even-toilet-based volcanos. Agnes has banished me and Dad to the sidelines while she sets up her own project, a gumball dispenser that demonstrates Newton's three laws of motion *and* the six simple machines. It's one of those wacky contraptions where you put in a quarter, and the quarter hits a lever, and seventy-five other things happen in a domino effect until the gumball comes out the other end.

My fourth-grade science fair project was a plant I accidentally scorched to death with a lamp.

I hope that Agnes's science fair project works better than the experiment we tried to launch on the drive over here: Operation Dress-Up Dad.

Hypothesis: Dad would be more attractive to Mom if he dressed better.

Required materials: Dad, some new clothes, a clue.

Procedure: From the shotgun seat, I announced, "Dad, you need new clothes."

Dad didn't even pause before shutting this down. "No, I don't."

Okay. Here, Dad was demonstrating Newton's first law of motion: A dad at rest stays at rest until you make him move.

"Dad, you'd look more handsome if you had

new clothes," said Agnes, applying force from the backseat.

Dad displayed the principle of resistance. "What's wrong with my clothes?"

I hit him with an equal and opposite reaction. "They're kind of old-fashioned-looking."

"I like them that way," said Dad, ending the conversation.

Conclusion: Dad isn't getting new clothes. Inertia wins again.

By the time Dad and I have made a full loop of the auditorium, Agnes has assembled her machine and is doing some test runs. A woman with dark hair and glasses is listening as Agnes explains her math. "The quarter weighs 5.7 grams, so that affects the weight of the lever and how far it needs to be from the fulcrum."

The woman nods. "Did you know that when you started, or did you discover that through trial and err—?"

"Trial and error," interrupts Dad. "Two things I'm great at." He extends his hand to the woman for a shake.

Ohhhhhhhh nooooooooooo. Everything goes slow-mo for a second as I imagine throwing my body in front of this lady so she doesn't get hit with the full force of Dad's corniness. But she's already reached out and taken his hand. *Toooooo laaaaaaate . . .*

She laughs as they shake. "Dan, right? I'm Tracy Rivera, Agnes's math and science teacher. We spoke by phone a couple of months ago . . ."

Agnes cringes and takes a few sideways steps so she's out of view.

"Oh, right," Dad remembers. "The potassium nitrate thing. Sorry again about that."

For something that could have blown up Agnes's school, Dad doesn't sound too sorry. And he certainly is looking at Ms. Rivera intently. This isn't his "lawyer" look. This is his "I forget sometimes that Dad is a guy until he gets this look" look. The one that makes me want to pluck my eyeballs out of my face and rinse them under cool, running water so they are clean again.

Agnes could help me out here, but she's sidled off to stand by the emergency exit. Good instinct, Agnes: When all else fails, set off an alarm and *run*.

I join her by the exit, rapidly updating her. "This is a catastrophe. Dad is flirting with your teacher. We have to put a stop to this."

Agnes peeks over at them. "They're just talking."

The *one time* Agnes plays dumb, and it has to be now. "No, they're not just talking. They're talking and smiling and looking in each other's eyes. And look, he touched her elbow! We have to do something!"

My eyes are locked on Dad and Ms. Rivera, but Agnes is more interested in watching a kid put a quarter in her gumball machine. Even if she doesn't win an award (which Agnes always does), she'll make a healthy profit in quarters. "What am I supposed to do about it?"

This should not take a genius to figure out.

"Get back over there! Distract them! Interrupt them!"

"Dad says I'm not supposed to interrupt," she contests.

"Well, he's not supposed to flirt with other people! He's a married man!"

Agnes goes back to stand by her project, while Dad and Ms. Rivera chat away. I give up and move on. There are some empty chairs over by the third graders, so I sit down near a kid whose "rat in a maze" project features gummy rats instead of real ones. ("The real rats escaped into the heating system, and now our whole house smells like grilled rat," he explains to a teacher.)

A familiar voice interrupts the rat saga. "Hey," says Harry Homework, out of nowhere. "Your sister goes here, right?"

"Hey!" I say. "Yeah. She's over there with my dad."

Harry takes a chair and pulls it up next to mine. I'm happy to see him. I forgot he has a younger brother in the grade below Agnes. He's probably sitting at one of these tables with a robot clone he built from scratch. "Where's your brother?"

"Anderson? He's over there." Harry points to a tiny red-haired kid with a dead plant and a desperate look. My heart goes out to young Anderson. I can tell we have a lot in common.

Harry's parents, Mr. and Mrs. Homework, are taking pictures of Anderson and his display. They're both short and thin, with wiry gray hair and glasses—one of those salt-and-pepper-shaker couples, where they look like a matched set and you can't imagine one without the other. Pretty much the opposite of "opposites attract."

"So," says Harry. "Are you going to the spring dance?"

I laugh out loud. Harry's hilarious. Why would I go to the spring dance? Dances are for popular people, not for wallflowers, and I'm as wallfloral as it gets. What's more, there might not even be a spring dance, unless I find a way for Sophie to replace the money.

"Why is that funny?" Harry looks hurt. "You *are* on the decorating committee."

Oh, right. He saw me in the lunchroom yesterday, sitting with all my besties on the deco com, discussing the scent-scape. "Yeah, but not 'cause I want to be. It's for business purposes."

"Oh."

Harry sounds disappointed. It occurs to me that he might be trying to ask for a dance-related favor. Maybe there's someone he likes, and he wants me to find out if they're interested. Maybe I can play Cupid for Harry. I'm still working on his bullying problem, but in the meantime I could help him with his romantic life.

"Why?" I ask. "Are you going?"

He looks down shyly at his shoes. "I might, if the right person says they'll go with me."

The right person. Okay. I don't know if he has anybody particular in mind, or if he's looking for help finding that person, but I'm already working on it. Who in our grade would be right for Harry?

It would have to be someone who (a) understands calculus and (b) likes younger guys. I'm drawing a blank on this, but I'll keep it in mind.

Speaking of romance, a quick glance tells me it might be time to run some more interference with Dad and Ms. Rivera, as she is hovering dangerously close to Agnes's display again.

"I gotta go keep my dad from making an ass of himself," I say, getting up from my seat. "See you Monday."

Harry extends his fist for me to bump. "See you."

Over by Agnes's project, Dad is busy being the Proud Parent, talking with everyone who comes by as though he built the machine. "There's a lot of math involved. You know, the quarter weighs a certain amount, so the lever has to weigh less than that..." Meanwhile, Agnes is counting all the quarters she's collected in a wooden box. She's made so much money in an hour, I'm thinking Sophie could probably solve her problem in a weekend with the right gumball machine.

Ms. Rivera is nearby, but fortunately, she's talking to some other parent. Unfortunately, Dad keeps looking over at her.

"Dad," I say. "Dad. Hey, Dad."

He's too busy staring at Agnes's teacher. I don't know why. She's pretty enough, and she seems nice, but she's nothing special. Not like Mom.

"DAD. Dad. Dad. Dad. DAD. Can we stop for food on the way home? Dad?" I keep this up until he acknowledges me, his *other* brilliant-genius daughter.

"Hmmm," he says absentmindedly. "Maybe you're right. Maybe I do need new clothes."

18

Sunday

I'm about to hang out at the mall with Sophie Nelson and my dad.

Now there's something I never thought I would say: *Just gonna chillax with Sophie and Dad at the mall.* But she needs money, and he needs serious help, so he's buying some of her expertise, like Baxter suggested. Maybe today Dad will purchase his first pair of jeans that aren't light blue and enormous.

Sophie is waiting for us by the Froyo place at noon, as we discussed last night. She's early, like she usually is—one of the things that makes everyone think she's perfect—and she's dressed up in her professional clothes (a blazer and skirt).

She smiles and waves as we approach. "Hiyee!"

I allow myself to be air-kissed. "Hey, Sophie. This is my dad. Dad, this is Sophie."

Fashion expert, meet fashion idiot. They shake hands.

"Is your mom joining us?" asks Dad. "Glad mentioned she might come along."

Sophie rolls her eyes. "She's already shopping. She couldn't wait."

The three of us sit down at a table to plan the attack. "I was thinking we'd start with the shoes, because they're the foundation," says Sophie. "Many dads only have two pairs—one pair of work shoes and one pair of sneakers—and that limits your versatility."

Dad is already impressed. "I have to say, Sophie, fashion consulting for parents is a great idea."

Aw, shucks. Thanks, Dad, I'm pretty proud of it myself. Though I did get some help from Baxter . . .

"Oh, thanks!" Sophie beams. "And thanks for being my first client."

Before we start walking around to stores, Sophie asks Dad a bunch of questions and records his answers in a little notebook. First she asks the practical questions, like his sizes and the colors and patterns he likes and dislikes. Then she gets into more abstract stuff. "What do you want your clothes to say?"

I wait for Dad to answer, *I want them to say, "Hello, I'm a shirt! Please wear me on your torso! I will keep you warm!"* But he spares us the hilarity this time. "I want them to say, 'You can trust me to help you with your complicated tax problem.'"

Sophie nods. "So they should say 'smart.'"

"Yes."

"'Responsible.'"

"That too."

"Even 'a little bit heroic.'"

"I suppose," Dad says, looking extremely pleased. "Sure."

Sophie finishes her questionnaire, and we head off to our first stop, a shoe store. "I see you've been wearing these shoes for a while," Sophie says tactfully. "What do you like about them? Okay, comfort . . . How about the style? And how would you feel about a more rounded toe?"

An hour later, we're back at the Froyo place, having a snack and people-watching. One of those overdone women with high heels and fake boobs and painted-on eyebrows is wobbling toward us, carrying a million shopping bags, and I am about to elbow my dad and smirk at her when the woman comes over to our table and drops her haul on the empty seat.

"Hi, baby! How's it going?"

Um, wow. This is Sophie's mom. She is very thin and very tan, and her long blond hair is very fake. She's wearing tight jeans and a sweater with a low neckline and lots of necklaces hanging down into her cleavage. Her forehead is smooth and shiny. Her swollen lips make her look like she got smacked in the mouth with an iron. I think there may even be eyes under all the mascara she has on.

Dad stands up, because a lady has approached a table where he is sitting, and that's the kind of thing Dad does—pops out of his seat anytime a woman comes over to his dining table, unless she's wearing a name tag and taking his order.

"Hi there," he says suavely. "I'm Gladys's father, Dan."

Sophie's mom bats her lashes, giving the mascara a workout. "I'm Gloria. So nice to meet you, Dan."

She leans over to shake his hand, and I have to stop putting Froyo in my mouth for a second so I can vomit at the way her cleavage is in Dad's face. This is *so heinous*. Also, *so mysterious*. Why is everyone suddenly flirting with Dad? Is he wearing new cologne? Because I will flush it right down the toilet and replace it with sour milk. I want Dad to be attractive to Mom, not to all these randos.

But I will say one thing for Sophie's mom: She *loves* her daughter. With *italics*. Sophie is all she talks about as she totters along in her heels next to

Dad on our way to the next stop. "Sophie's an only child," Gloria explains. "And I raised her alone. So we're very close. She's my whole life."

"Of course," agrees Dad, like I'm his whole life, too. Please. We both know that I'm, at best, 33.3 percent of my father's life.

"Everything Sophie does, she excels at. I can't tell you how proud I am. She said she wanted to run for the student council, and I said, 'But what about the dance squad? They need you, they're nothing without you!' And she says, 'No problem, Mommy, I can do both.'"

"Mommy" continues blathering on about her amazing daughter. Blah, blah, Sophie's so special. She's so talented. She's so popular at school. She's the greatest dancer. *And a klepto!* Don't forget that.

I wish there was something about me that Dad could brag about—some award, some grades, some social triumph—but I remain average in every way. "I'm so proud of Glad. She . . . goes to school!" If Agnes was here, Dad could brag about her, but she's at the roller rink with her friend Miranda. It doesn't matter anyway, because Gloria is nowhere near finished raving about Sophie.

"And now she wants to do this fashion-consulting thing? I think it's a great idea. She could turn it into a real business. Maybe give her mom a job, ha-ha."

Dad takes this seriously and immediately dorks out. "Well, if Sophie wants to incorporate, I'd be happy to advise her. She could form what's called a Delaware S corp—of course, you'd have to be the one to sign the paperwork, but . . ."

He goes on to offer advice about "DBAs," "LLCs," and a bunch of other meaningless letters. Gloria listens as though he is speaking English, and Sophie and I trail behind them.

Sophie's been chattering this whole time about her friends and their love lives. "Carolina and Hannah were supposed to hang out with Will and Amir, but both the guys like Carolina, and both the girls like Amir, so it's like, who's going to be with who? I feel bad for Hannah; everybody always likes Carolina more. Of course, Carolina's a total tease—that's what Amir told me. And I'm like, 'Then why do you like her?' And he's like, 'She's hot.' And I'm like, 'Then why were you texting with Desiree?' Because Desiree told me last week . . ."

I'm wondering why she's telling me all this personal stuff about her friends. Then I get it: Sophie is gossiping with me. And Sophie gossiping with me is like Izzy punching me in the arm. It's how you know you're her friend.

So this is what people mean by "girl talk." I'm kind of enjoying it. I love having information I'm not supposed to have, and I certainly am learning a lot—I had no idea the A+ table was such a fiery hotbed of drama. Student council president Rich Savoy confessed his love for Carolina, who rejected him, and now they're ignoring each other! Desiree is playing both sides of the unspoken Carolina-Hannah war! What fun!

We keep shopping for another half hour until Dad's inner accountant takes over and he becomes physically unable to spend a single dime more.

Gloria smooths the front of a sweater over his chest and remarks on its softness—the sweater, not Dad's chest, ha-ha!—but even that cannot break the curse. So she puts the sweater back and picks up her shopping bags, and we are walking out of the store when the alarm goes off.

The security guard doesn't look too concerned as he ambles over. This happens all the time—a cashier forgets to take the magnetic tag off an item—no big deal. Half the time, it's an item from another store anyway. Dad stops obligingly to show the guard the contents of his shopping bags.

The guard reaches into one of the bags and takes out a pair of sunglasses with the store's tag on them. Dad looks stumped at the sight. He didn't try on any sunglasses today. "How did those get in there?" Dad asks.

The guard frowns at Dad. "Sir, I need to ask you the same question."

"Well, I have no idea." Dad shrugs. "Glad you caught it, though."

We're ready to leave, but the guard is blocking our way. "So you have no idea why you were walking out with a pair of sunglasses from our store."

"Oh, I wasn't trying to take them!" Dad protests. He laughs at the idea. "It's a misunderstanding. I honestly have no idea how they got there."

Gloria steps forward. "It was obviously an accident," she says, annoyed. "We were trying things on, they must have got knocked into one of the bags by mistake."

The guard gets a look at Gloria in all her glory, then he reevaluates Dad. Other people are looking, too, and I want to hide under a rack of shirts. Does the guard think Dad and Gloria are married? Do these people think this creature is my mom? Now *that* is a misunderstanding. I look at Sophie, my assumed sister, but she won't meet my eyes.

Suddenly I realize how the sunglasses got in Dad's bag.

Gloria continues her argument. I can't tell if

she knows about Sophie's stealing problem and she's trying to cover for her daughter or if she honestly thinks this was a mistake. "You have the glasses, we obviously weren't trying to take them, we're done here." She shoves past the guard and out the door, and we follow.

Dad stops by the escalator and marvels at the experience. "That has never happened to me before. I have never been accused of stealing before. How strange."

Gloria puts her hand on his arm in sympathy. "It's ridiculous that anybody would think that! Things get knocked over all the time, especially when you've got narrow aisles like they do. That store is too crowded, that's the problem. Stuff falling everywhere . . ."

Sophie stands there wide-eyed and innocent, as though she didn't just set my dad up for a misdemeanor. Ironically, Dad turns and thanks her.

"Well, it was a pleasure to meet you, Sophie, and thank you so much. Your fee was $15 an hour, and we did two and a half hours, so I owe you $37.50. We'll make it an even $40." He digs out his wallet and hands Sophie two twenties.

"Thanks so much," she gushes. "I hope you'll love your new look."

"And, Gloria," says Dad, in an entirely different tone of voice, "what a *great* pleasure to meet you. You have my card—please let me know if I can advise you on any, uh, business matters, or anything."

"Oh, absolutely!" Gloria presses one hand to her heart to express her sincerity. "And Gladys, please come over anytime. Sophie and I would love that."

Yeah, Sophie would loooooooooove that. I give her the evil eye, which she repels by not looking at me. "Thanks," I say sweetly to Gloria. "That sounds great."

Dad and I split off from the Nelsons, head outside, and walk through the parking lot to our car. He puts the bags in the trunk and slams it shut with gusto. "There," he says proudly. "New clothes."

He hums a jaunty little tune on the drive home. "I'm glad you're making friends like Sophie," he pronounces, turning on to our block. "She's a very accomplished young lady."

I close my eyes for a second so they don't bulge out of my head. Deep breath in, long breath out.

"Yep." I sigh. "She sure is something."

19

Monday Morning

When the doorbell rings at 7:45 a.m.,
I am ready by the door.

"It's for me!" I yell. "I got it!"

I told Dad that my friend Izzy is going to start coming by in the mornings to walk with me to the bus. Of course he said yes—another new friend, hallelujah! Between Sophie and Izzy, I might even have enough people for a birthday party this year. I wonder what Dad will think when he sees what I see when I open the door.

A girl I've never met before stands there, her chin-length hair curled and her earrings dangling. On her feet are dainty silver flats with bows on them; around her wrist is a charm bracelet. She appears to have fashioned a crude cloak out of a fleece blanket that says GO ELMHAVEN in the school colors, light blue and maroon, and she is trying very hard to cover her entire self with it.

"Hey," Izzy says miserably.

"Hey!" I try to control my face and react normally, but it's a little like opening the door and seeing someone dressed in a gorilla costume. "Hey, come on in, you can put your stuff down here."

I want to rush her through the house without a long interview with my dad, who will undoubtedly embarrass me. But he's on the phone, so he just waves from the kitchen, and Izzy waves back, clutching her cloak around her with one hand. Agnes and Mabey pop their heads out from the kitchen and say hi, then go back to their English muffins.

"Let's go upstairs," I suggest.

Izzy and I tromp up to my room. Her clothes are hung up neatly in my closet, and she groans with relief when she sees them. Then she lets the cloak drop, and I get a look at her in the clothes her grandma bought her, and I groan, too—in agony.

There is a blouse. It is a pink button-down with a rounded collar and an embroidered butterfly on the chest. There is a skirt. It is lavender and knee length and it puffs out like a triangle. There are pink tights that sparkle, and for me, it is these sparkling tights that officially put this outfit into the category of "cruel and unusual punishment."

"Oh. My . . ."

"I know." Izzy is already stripping off the tights and ripping out the earrings. "I can't believe I survived the shopping trip. I have never heaved so much in my life. Not even after that hot dog–eating contest last fall. I *like* hot dogs."

I turn away to play a game on my phone while she gets dressed, which takes no time at all. Within two minutes, the Izzy I know is back, standing in my bedroom.

She's in a faded T-shirt and her most weathered jeans. Her cruddy red sneakers have replaced the flats. Her curled hair is hidden under her cap. There's still pink polish on her nails, and she smells like a petunia in full bloom, but otherwise, she's back to looking like herself.

"Ahhhhhhhhhhh," she says.

I have never heard such a contented sigh. It's like a commercial for arthritis medicine, where some old person is in horrible pain until they take the pill, and then they're all blissed out because they're not in searing agony anymore and they can garden again.

Izzy takes the skirt and blouse and tights, those glittery horrors, and starts folding them into her softball duffel, along with her fleece cloak and dainty shoes. "I would be dying right now, I swear. You're literally saving my life."

The zipper strains against the fleece, but she gets it closed.

"No problem."

I get my stuff together, and we go back downstairs. I yell "BYE!" as we pass the kitchen entryway, then we head out for the bus.

We fall silent as we walk. I'd been wondering what I could talk about with Izzy. I don't play soccer or softball, and I don't watch sports on TV. I'm not sure what else she likes, besides incredibly shabby clothes.

"So I'm not gay," says Izzy abruptly. "In case you were wondering."

Well *there's* a conversation starter for you.

"Okay."

Izzy kicks at a rock on the sidewalk. "I know that's what people think. Everyone just assumes I'm gay. Even my dad and stepmom. I'm not anything! Why is that hard to understand? I don't want to kiss a girl *or* a boy. I'm just not interested."

Yes!

"Me neither," I say.

Izzy's declaration comes as an incredible relief. Lately I've felt like everybody else in our grade is interested in dating, except me. Liz Kotlinski has parties at her house where they play truth or dare and spin the bottle and whatever the whatever—I only know this because of the many fixing jobs that have resulted from those games, most of them failures. Sadly, you can't un-kiss someone, or un–take off your shirt.

It turns out Izzy and I have something else in common: Her mom left her and her dad a few years ago. Now her dad is remarried to Ashley, and Izzy's mom lives in Massachusetts with Izzy's other grandma, who has dementia. Izzy only sees her mom and grandma a few times a year, and it's always really weird and depressing.

"Do you miss your mom?" I ask.

Izzy shrugs. "I don't think about it that much."

Oh, me neither. I almost never think about my mom. I only spend most of my waking life trying to find a way to get her back home.

When the bus comes, I get on and stop at an empty seat near the front. Izzy hesitates just a step, then continues on without me, punching a few people on her way down the aisle and calling them jackweeds. She drops into an open seat next to Jackson.

"What's that smell?" I hear him ask. There's an uncomfortably long pause.

I'm about to turn around and take credit for the perfume, when Izzy says, "That's the smell of athletic ability, son! That's why you don't recognize it."

High fives and arm punches for everyone. Izzy calls them all jackweeds a few more times, and I smile to myself, alone in my uncool front-of-the-bus seat.

Izzy's friends might not know it, but I'm a jackweed, too.

20

Monday Lunch

I am ducking Sophie Nelson by hiding in the resource room.

I am also ducking Madison Graham. And Ms. Schellestede. And Taye, who's been trying to get me to do another favor. And Rebba-Becky Lewis. Basically, I am hiding from everyone. Or so I think.

"There you are!"

Sophie plops down in the seat next to me and lowers her voice. "Hey, girl, I was looking for you all morning. Where were you?"

On the corner of Avoiding Street and You Avenue. That's what I'd say if I felt the need to answer her question, which I do not.

"What do you want?" I ask coldly.

If she notices my unfriendly tone, she doesn't show it. She gets right down to business in her usual peppy voice. "Okay, the thing with your dad was great, but we have to get money faster. The council's going to need it by Friday—"

Mind = boggled. Sophie has *got* to be kidding me. She thinks I'm still going to help her? I'm actually impressed by how insanely bossy she is. I'm too shy to ask a waitress for more ketchup, but Sophie has no problem demanding that I continue to bail her out of trouble after she gets my dad accused of stealing, despite everything I've already done for her.

I cut her off. "Sophie. The thing with my dad was not great."

"What?" Her eyes widen with surprise. "He wasn't happy with his new look? I thought the sweater-vests were killer on him. They really broaden the shoulders, and the patterns are so fun . . ."

She spews more fashion blather like nothing's

wrong, but I'm not going to let her get away with playing dumb. "Sophie. There was a pair of sunglasses in my dad's shopping bag that he didn't pay for, and you put them there."

Sophie looks shocked. "No, I didn't."

She says it so believably, I almost buy her denial. I guess I could have made a mistake—maybe it really was an accident that knocked the sunglasses into Dad's bag. But it seems way more likely that Sophie, who steals things, tried to steal them. I study her face, and she gazes back at me innocently. *Too* innocently. If she tries to open her eyes any wider, she will sprain her forehead. "Sophie."

"I swear! It must have been an accident, like my mom said."

"Of course. Or maybe your 'friend' took them."

I look directly into her eyes, but she barely flinches. If I thought the mention of her "friend" would break her, I was wrong.

Here's a professional tip: The only way to pass a lie-detector test when you're guilty is to convince yourself of your own innocence. For instance, Sophie can't be caught in a lie if she believes what she says is the truth. So it looks like Sophie has convinced herself that there really is some "friend" who took the money, just like Madison convinced herself that "James" is real.

Breaking news: I am surrounded by lunatics.

"Nobody took the glasses!" Sophie laughs. "Nothing happened. Everything was fine."

Well, if she's going to deny reality, I'm going to deny it, too. "Okay, so everything is fine, then."

I turn away from her and go back to my phone. *We're done here.*

Sophie sits and watches me for a minute while I full-strength ignore her. Finally, she reaches out and puts her hand on my arm. "But we still need to replace the money."

I jerk my arm away from her touch. "No, Sophie, *we* do not need to do anything." If we weren't in the resource room, I'd be yelling, but I'm forced to keep my voice down to an enraged hiss. "I did everything I could for you. I gave you a way to stall for time. I gave you an idea for making money. I even got you your first customer. Now *you* need to replace the money. That *you* took."

Boom. There it is, out in the open: the truth. It gasps and writhes painfully in front of us like a fish on land, suffocating on the silence.

Sophie's lips are pressed together in a tight white line. She flattens her hands on the table and looks at them, flexing her fingers to admire her manicure. Thinking.

"They're going to expel me, aren't they?"

She asks this normally, without excess emotion, as if she's asking, *Is this nail polish bluish purple or purplish blue?* Just confirming a minor fact: She's going to get expelled from school. And she's going to lose all her friends. Obviously, Sophie didn't consider the consequences when she took the money.

I don't want to consider them, either. "I don't know."

Sophie continues looking at her hands, still eerily calm. "They could arrest me."

The idea makes me shudder. I wish I could say, *Oh, no, that probably won't happen, you'll be okay.* But I think Sophie might be right. Unless she can replace the money, she could be charged with theft. In which case, the school will probably call the police.

"This will follow me for the rest of my life." She looks up from her nails, finally, and her eyes are watery. She tries to smile, but only one corner of her mouth lifts. "Thanks for trying to help, Glad. I'm sorry about the sunglasses."

All right, fine. I know I shouldn't feel sorry for her, but my heart sinks at the thought of Sophie in handcuffs. I'm scared for her—more scared than she seems for herself. If Sophie gets arrested, her life is basically over. I don't know if I can live with that on my conscience.

"Okay, you're right. Fashion consulting won't get you the money fast enough. There has to be another way to get it."

My mind starts grinding. If I were in danger of being arrested, what would I do? No question, I'd go to my dad. Even though he'd kill me. "Why don't you ask your mom?"

Sophie shakes her head. "I can't."

"Why not?" I think of Gloria's many shopping bags—surely she has enough money to keep her daughter from getting arrested. And it's obvious that she would never say no to Sophie.

"I don't know if you heard, but I'm her whole life." Sophie smiles sadly at the backs of her hands. "That's what she's always telling people, and it's true. She has no life of her own. Every single thing I do, she's standing there watching, waiting for me to do something she can brag about. She's like, 'Oh, Sophie got invited to two parties at the same time this weekend.' I'm like, 'Mom, the gas station guy doesn't care.' But she wants me to have this perfect life, so I have to be perfect."

A mom who's too involved in her daughter's life. Hmmm. I try to imagine what this must be like.

Sophie's eyes shine with tears. "Please, Glad. Please help me figure out how to get this money."

Sucker, party of one.

"I will, if I can," I say honestly. "But I don't know what I can do. Everybody in the world is trying to figure out how to get money. But I'll think about it some more. That's all I can promise."

Sophie nods. She takes in a deep breath and lets it out. "Thanks," she says. "You're a good friend, Glad."

I don't know if she means I'm *her* good friend, or if I'm just "a good friend" in general, the way Izzy is "a good batter," or Evelyn Ferszt is "a good reason to fear for your life." But she's right: Carolina has nothing on me. Dance squad captain Carolina Figgis, with the friends and the clothes and the looks and the attitude, has been Sophie's BFF for ages, the two of them involved in all the same activities, sharing their most precious memories. And she still can't touch me.

Right now, I'm the best friend Sophie has.

21

Monday After School

I'm sitting with Harry on a bench outside school, reviewing his case while he waits for his ride.

Harry's distracted, though, and he won't stick to the subject. He interrupts me in the middle of my analysis of his adversaries. "Where were you at lunch today?"

"Business," I tell him.

He nods, looking off into the distance. "I thought maybe you were sitting with your new friends again, but I didn't see you at their table."

Har-har, I'm about to say, but he's not kidding.

"They're not my new friends."

"Ah." Harry clears his throat. "Well, I wanted to ask . . ."

A burnout eighth grader named Declan passes our bench, shooting a look at Harry like an angry boss who caught his employee goofing off. *Harrison, I want that report on the North American explorers on my desk by tomorrow morning!*

I stare back at Declan with a look that says, *I know what you keep in your locker, and if you even think about coming over here, I'll make sure Ms. Schellestede knows, too.*

Harry is too busy phrasing his question to catch this wordless exchange, and I am too oblivious to stop him from asking it. "I mean, I thought maybe . . . I was wondering . . . Will you go to the spring dance with me?"

Oh, no. Oh, no no no no no no no. Oh, please, God, don't let Harry like me. PLEASE. Please don't make me hurt his feelings like this. Please don't let me lose one of the few friends I've got. And—oh, dear God—*please* don't tell me he was trying to ask me to the dance at Agnes's science fair, when I walked away before he could finish his sentence.

I haven't said a word, but the look on my face must say it all, because I can see the disappointment on Harry's.

"Never mind," he says, blushing furiously as he stands to leave.

"Wait, Harry . . ." He pauses to hear me out, but I can't finish my sentence. Wait for what? For me to fall in love with him? For me to want to go on a romantic date with anybody ever? For time to go backward, so I can run away with my hands over my ears before he asks me out?

Harry turns away. "Forget it. This was a mistake." He doesn't look back as he walks off to his ride.

I want to go after him, but I know there's no use. I bury my face in my hands and press the heels of my palms into my eyes and watch the shifting lights and shadows. If only there were someone I could go to who could fix this problem, the way people come to me.

Taye is the first thing I see when I open my eyes. He's coming toward me with *I need another favor* on his face, looking around to make sure nobody's paying attention as he approaches. I stand to walk away, but he's already in front of me.

"Hey," he says. "I need a—"

Yeah, you can stop right there. Unless you need an *I don't care*—I have plenty of those!—I can't help you. I'm done for the day. The doctor is out. The store is closed. *Cerrado*. It's time for me to get on my bus.

"Not now," I say, brushing past him.

Yet Taye follows me. "But I—"

Nope. "Not now," I repeat, louder this time.

"But—"

ARGH. Is *not now* hard to comprehend? Can Taye only hear things when cheerleaders say them? Because I will spell it out for him, dance squad–style. *N* to the *O* to the *T*! *N* to the *O* to the *W*!

"NOT. NOW. TAYE."

My raised voice causes a few looks.

There's a flash of panic in Taye's eyes, then he backs away from me, wrinkling his nose like, *Ew, Glad.* "Fine, then. Freak."

Someone nearby laughs, and it hits me like a punch in the stomach. Taye has just been upgraded from "not now" to "not ever."

I go straight to the bus, slip gratefully into a seat by the front, and let my head rest against the window. Once again, people are outside in little clusters, laughing with their friends, and I'm hiding here on the bus alone, because I'm a *freak*.

I keep my head against the window as the bus leaves, and it stays there for the whole ride home. Izzy, Taye, and the other sportsballers have a game today, so the bus is only half-full, and it's quiet enough to think. Quiet enough to hear Taye's voice saying over and over in my head: *freak*.

Everything's telling me it's time to get out of the game. It's not worth the trouble anymore. Schellestede's on my case, Madison's gone bonkers, Sophie's made me an accessory to her crimes, and

I'm losing my appetite for other people's problems. Even worse, I might be losing my touch. I spent literally hours working on a plan to keep Harry from getting hurt at school. And then I turned around and hurt him.

Hurting Harry—that's the worst part. I hear Taye's voice, but I see Harry's face, turning away from me. *Forget it. This was a mistake.* Yeah. Mistakes are all I make these days. As hard as I tried, I didn't make things better for my friend at all. In fact, I actively made things worse. And now I've lost the closest thing I had to a partner in crime.

Some help I am.

22

Tuesday Morning

Dad is in way too good a mood today:

1. He's been singing, and not just in the shower.
2. ALL MORNING.
3. It's that corny old song called "Walking on Sunshine."

He continues to hum at the breakfast table, in between slurping his coffee. *"Hmmmm hmmm hmmm."* *Sssslllluurrppp.* *"And don't it feel GOOD!"* *Sssssllll-luuuurppp.* Mabey looks like she's going to strangle him. I'm happy that Dad's happy, but I hope he's done singing by the time Izzy gets here.

Mabey flat-out asks him: "Why are you so happy today?"

Dad puts down his tablet, pleased by the question. "'Cause I look so good in my new clothes. Look, these are my black 'skinny jeans.' I can dress them up with a blazer and tie, or I can be casual in them." He gets up and strikes a catwalk pose. "See?"

He's making fun of himself and the whole fashion-makeover thing, but I can tell he is also kind of proud of his outfit. He does look better without the enormous pleated khakis. He looks like a TV dad. Sophie's right, the sweater-vest makes his shoulders look broader, and the tailored shirt underneath makes him look less stuffy.

"Which reminds me, I need my hat." Dad hops up the stairs to his room, singing all the way.

Mabey and I look at each other, mystified. "Okay," Mabey says quietly. "I know he likes his new clothes, but what is up with the singing?"

"I have no idea." I shrug.

Agnes has a hypothesis: "I think he's going to ask out Ms. Rivera."

My leg starts jiggling uncontrollably under the table.

"What?" Mabey hisses, outraged. "That's stupid, why would you say that?"

Agnes scowls at the word *stupid* and answers the question in her haughtiest manner. "Well, for one thing, last night he asked me a bunch of questions about her, like how old she is, whether she has kids..."

I *knew* this was going to be a problem. I called it. Agnes should have helped me torpedo their conversation on Saturday, but she was too busy being a gumball mogul. And she sounds pretty unconcerned now, as she continues.

"And then he said he was going to pick me up from school today instead of Baxter. I think he's going to ask her then."

Yeah, Agnes isn't sounding nearly as upset as she should, but Mabey makes up for it by being extra-upset. "No way," says Mabey, teeth clenched. Her leg joins mine at the under-table jiggle party. "He *can't*."

I hope Mom gets her plane ticket *soon*.

Dad's singing gets closer as he comes down the stairs. He re-enters the kitchen with his new hat sitting at a rakish angle on his head. "This is called a trilby," he informs us. "Not a fedora. See, it's got a narrower brim." He steps back into the hall to check himself out in the mirror.

"It looks dumb," mutters Mabey. She slinks away to her room to get her stuff.

Agnes puts her dishes in the dishwasher and goes to the hall for her shoes and coat. "I like it," she offers.

"Thank you," says Dad, frowning at his own reflection like a tough guy, then raising one eyebrow. He leans in to see his beard better, running a hand over it like he's rethinking its presence on his face.

If this makeover gets Dad to shave his beard, it will be worth all the trouble I've gone through for Sophie.

Correction: the trouble I continue to go through for Sophie.

Finally, Dad tears himself away from the mirror, and he and Agnes depart for her school. "Bye, love you, Mabes Babes!" he calls on the way out the door. "Bye, love you, BunBun!"

I am *so grateful* Izzy missed that.

She didn't miss it by much. A minute later, Izzy arrives, clutching her cloak around her like Little Fleece Riding Hood. I don't know how she runs from her place to mine in girly shoes while wrapped in a blanket, but I bet it's an extraordinary sight. The local kids are going to grow up telling campfire stories about *the blue-and-maroon ghost who traveled swiftly over the land after sunrise.*

"Hey," huffs Izzy, breathless from her workout, as I let her in. "Thanks again for letting me do this."

She follows me upstairs to my room and drops her cloak. Today's blouse is somehow even pinker than yesterday's, and the skirt is an eggy yellow with tulips on it. I want to look away in self-protection, but I'm mesmerized by the horror.

"I KNOW," she says, seeing my face.

Oops. "Sorry."

She sighs, grabbing a sweatshirt and jeans. "Not as sorry as I am."

I avert my eyes while she changes her clothes, looking around my side of the room. I try to see it through Izzy's eyes and I cringe. I'm so basic and boring, with my alphabetized books, my shoes all lined up neatly in a row.

"Look at you in Disney World." Izzy's finished changing, and she's looking at an old photo on my bulletin board—me, Mabey, and Agnes posing in front of the castle, wearing ridiculous hats. I curse myself for overlooking it when I was purging my room of kiddie stuff. "Wow." She looks from the picture to me to the picture. "You look so different here."

I sincerely hope I'm not turning red. "Yeah. I was eight. And wearing a princess hat." I take a step toward the door, ready to leave, but Izzy lingers in front of the bulletin board.

"No, I mean, you look so happy." Now she's looking at a picture of the five of us, taken in Grandma June's backyard, all of us smiling hugely. I'm definitely taking those pictures down ASAP. In fact, let's get rid of the whole bulletin board. "You never smile like that. You're always so intense."

Intense. I wonder if that's good or bad.

Izzy tries to clarify it. "You're, like, always really focused. Instead of being social, or whatever. You don't ever just hang out with people. You gotta hang out more."

Trust me, I want to hang out. Izzy is so effortlessly popular, she thinks popularity is easy to come by. Like I could be just as popular as her if I chose to be. "People don't invite me to hang out."

She tears herself away from the bulletin board and begins packing up her tulip-covered clothes. "That's because they're scared of you."

My eyes bug halfway out of their sockets. Izzy has got to be kidding. The only scary thing about me is my morning breath. "Scared of me?"

"Yeah," she says, with an implied *no duh*. "Why are you surprised? You know everything about everybody. You could tell other people their secrets anytime you want."

I grimace, nauseated by the very idea. If I gave away people's secrets, they would all get in trouble, and they would all hate me forever—the exact opposite of what I'm going for. "I would never."

"And you have this way of coming up with ideas nobody else would think of," Izzy continues. "It's almost spooky. Like when you told me to get clothes from the thrift store to fake out my grandma—how did you even think of that?"

To be honest, I don't really know how I think of these things. I've been doing it for so long, it feels automatic to me. People come to me with a problem, I concentrate for a few minutes, and I come up with an idea. Izzy's right—it is almost spooky.

So I shrug and mumble, "I dunno. Anyway, we should probably get going . . ."

Izzy changes the subject as we walk to the bus.

Now she's raving about this video game called *Kill War* or *Death Murder* or *Homicide Assault* or something. "And when you run a guy over with your tank, it's like a tube of toothpaste: He bulges, and his guts squish right out of his mouth . . ."

She continues her bloodthirsty ramblings until the bus comes, then she gets on and throws a few punches at her jackweed friends on her way down the aisle. When she sits next to Jackson, she lifts one butt cheek and rips a massive, burbling fart.

"FAIRY DUST!" she yells, as everyone nearby pulls the neck of their shirt over their nose to block the stench.

And *that*, apparently, is what it takes to be popular.

23

Tuesday After School

This school day *would not end.* It was *eternal.* You know how every year of a dog's life is supposed to be equal to seven human years? *Every hour of this day* was equal to seven human years. By fourth period, I felt like I was in my forties.

I couldn't even look at Harry all morning— meanwhile, Madison couldn't stop looking at me. At one point, she caught my eye and actually dragged her finger across her throat, which I'm pretty sure is against our school's aardvark-enforced anti-bullying policy.

At lunch, I hid in an unlocked classroom, lights off, alert for the sound of potential intruders. I needed to be alone. Every time I saw Rebba-Becky Lewis, or anybody else who looked like they wanted a favor, I ducked, and when I noticed Taye coming toward me between classes, an apologetic look on his face, I casually walked backward into the girls' room.

Sophie's the only one I spoke to. We rendez-voused by the third-floor teachers' bathroom before eighth period. After another fruitless night trying to think of get-cash-quick schemes, I'd come to the conclusion that she could either (a) try to sell one of her kidneys on eBay or (b) confess to her mom and ask her to front the money.

"Your mom will forgive you," I argued. "You know she will. And it's better than being arrested."

But I couldn't get Sophie to save her own neck. Yesterday in the resource room, I thought she and I had come to an understanding; today she was back to living in her dream world, where she hadn't done anything wrong. She drew back at the word *arrested* and made a face like I was being overdramatic.

"It'll be fine," she said, giving my arm a reassuring pat. "Mistakes happen, the bank could've lost it, you never know . . ."

Mistakes happen? Seriously? That was her strategy now? "Sophie. Banks don't lose people's money. When you put money in an account, it stays there."

She rolled her eyes as though I was being difficult. "Well . . . what if someone raided my account? Like identity theft?"

I couldn't even begin to list the ways in which this idea was terrible. And her sudden change in attitude was baffling. Why was she acting like this was no big deal? She was days away from getting in massive trouble. I was sweating several buckets over the punishment she was going to face. How could she be so cool about it?

"There you are!"

Carolina appeared at Sophie's side, giving me a big fake smile. (Hers, BTW, is not the kind of fake smile where you're actually trying to fool the other person. Hers is a "look at my fake smile" fake smile.)

She took Sophie's arm in hers. "What are you talking to *her* for?"

"Decorating," said Sophie casually. She waved her fingers at me to say goodbye, and Carolina led her away.

Fiiiiiiiiiiiiiinally. It's 3 p.m. I don't want to deal with anybody who might be looking for me outside, so I don't go straight for my bus—I dawdle for a while after my last class, lingering in Mr. Radford's room, taking a long time to pack up my stuff. I get my coat from my locker, and I'm just closing the lock when I see our music teacher, Mr. Gerber, walking straight toward me.

I don't know why Gerber would be coming for me, but I can see from his pace that it isn't good. My heart starts knocking against my rib cage like it's trying to get out.

Gerber stops, forehead furrowed, floppy hair sticking with sweat. "Gladys, have you seen Jasmine this afternoon?"

Knock knock, says my heart, but this is no joke. There is no good reason for Gerber to ask me about Jasmine's whereabouts. I'm not in the band. I'm not friends with Jasmine. I barely know the girl. I'm just the one who came up with her excuses.

"No," I squeak. "Sorry."

"She didn't text you?" he asks impatiently.

BANG BANG BANG BANG BANG. My heart is now a prisoner banging its metal cup against the bars of my ribs. "No."

I hold my phone out to him in case he wants to check, but he doesn't take it. I wish he would. It's true: I haven't seen or heard from Jasmine today. She hasn't texted me, today or any other day. But I'd still fail a lie-detector test, that's how scared and guilty I feel. They wouldn't even be able to stick the sensors to my skin, I'm sweating so much.

"So you have no idea where she is right now." His arms are folded and his expression is dubious. Like everyone else in school, I usually don't take

Gerber that seriously, but he is scaring the actual crap out of me right now.

I stumble on my words. "H-honestly, n-no, I haven't seen her. Last time I talked to her was . . . Thursday morning."

Thursday morning, when she needed another emergency excuse for missing band. When she seemed nervous for no reason, and I got a bad feeling about it. Well, that bad feeling is back, and it brought a bunch of friends, and I am now hosting several very bad feelings at once.

Gerber gives me more side-eye, but I think he can tell I'm sincere. If I knew where she was right now, I would be telling him, that's how freaked out I am. I want to ask, *Is Jasmine in trouble?* But the answer is all too obvious.

"If you see or hear from her," says Gerber before walking away, "tell her to get to practice today or she's cut from the band."

I stand there in the hall for a minute while my stomach threatens to send my half-digested lunch back up through my esophagus. I need to go catch my bus and ride far away from where I am currently standing, but my concrete legs don't want to move. It's only the sound of Ms. Schellestede's voice coming down the hallway that gets me to spring into action and sprint outside and across the courtyard, throwing myself through the bus door just in time for its departure.

I can't catch my breath for the whole ride home, and it's not just the sprint that has me winded. It's the pressure. I can't take it anymore. After my chat with Mr. Gerber, I'm afraid Jasmine might be in real trouble. I *know* Sophie is. And I've been mixed up in their trouble. Which means that some of it could splash back onto me.

Did I get transported into Izzy's war game somehow? Because right now, it feels like there's a tank rolling over me and all my guts are getting squished out like toothpaste.

24

Tuesday Night

We have assembled for an emer-gency meeting in the attic.

"Dad asked Ms. Rivera on a date," reports Agnes from her seat on the magnet-strewn floor. She leaves the *Just like I told you* part unspoken, but we can still clearly hear it. "She said no."

Mabey and I look at each other with alarm across the littered landscape of her room. This is all wrong—Dad should not be asking anybody on any dates! What is he thinking? He should be trying to work things out with Mom! He can't start dating other people! He didn't even discuss it with his daughters first!

At least he got shot down. I figured that's what happened, but I'm grateful for the confirmation. Dad was in a bad mood earlier, when he and Agnes got home, and I took that as a good sign—no more "Walking on Sunshine." Then he and Agnes played chess in near silence until the delivery guy showed up with our dinner, so we couldn't get the story out of her until now.

"Were you there?" Mabey presses. "Did you hear their conversation?"

Agnes arranges her magnets in some unknowable order on the floor. "Part of it. He was waiting in the hall when class got out, and then they were talking in the classroom while everybody was leaving, but then Dad told me to use the restroom before we left."

So you hung out in the hallway with your ear pressed to the door, right? That's what I'd have done. But Agnes, who is not a Master Eavesdropper like me, actually went to the bathroom. SMH.

"What'd you hear, then?" Mabey asks, nervously

twisting a lock of her hair. "How do you know she said no?"

There's a chorus of clacking sounds as Agnes uses one magnet to attract the others. "'Cause after I came back, I heard her say she has a policy against dating parents. She said it's too confusing for the kids."

Mabey and I exchange another *phew*. Ms. Rivera's dating policy for the win!

"We still need to fix him up," I reminded them. "The new clothes are good, but Mom's visiting soon, and he needs drastic personality changes."

Agnes looks up at me. "Do *you* think she's really going to come?"

Me? Yeah . . . I mean, right? "I do."

"Of course she's coming," Mabey says irritably. "She's been planning this for months. She's just working on the final details."

Agnes is silent.

"We could try calling her again," I suggest. "Agnes, you could talk to her this time."

Agnes goes back to her clacking. "That's okay," she mumbles at the floor.

Mabey makes a dismissive noise. "Fine. If you don't believe Mom, then you can leave. Glad and I can plan without you."

Agnes looks hurt as she gets up from the floor and collects her magnets. I hate when she and Mabey argue and I'm stuck in the middle. "No, stay . . . ," I say to Agnes, but she goes over to the hatch.

She pauses for a second before opening it. "I wish Ms. Rivera had said yes to Dad."

I gasp. "Agnes!"

Mabey springs to her feet. "GET OUT!" she yells.

"Fine," Agnes says in her prissiest voice. She opens the hatch. "I don't want to be here anyway."

Mabey's face is a furious red. "GET OUT OF MY ROOM!"

"GIRLS?" Dad yells from downstairs.

The three of us all yell back at the same time.

"NOTHING!"

"IT'S OKAY!"

"WE'RE FINE!"

No answer. Good. Agnes exits through the
hatch and Mabey lets it close heavily behind her.

She throws herself back onto her bed, flinging
one forearm over her eyes in a pose of dramatic
suffering. "I can't believe her," she begins. "I told
you we shouldn't have told her anything. She's so
annoying—she's just like Dad, she always has to
have the last word . . ."

"Mmm," I murmur supportively. "Uh-huh."

Meanwhile, I'm weighing my options. Mabey
needs me to stick around so she can vent about
Agnes and Dad. Agnes is probably downstairs in her
lab waiting for me to join her so she can complain
about Mabey and Mom. Which side am I on?

"I have homework," I say abruptly, getting up
to go.

Mabey stops mid-sentence and looks right at
me. I don't want to meet her eyes.

"Mom *is* coming," she says. "You do know that, right?"

The strain in her voice is painful to hear. If Mom bails, and Agnes says *I told you so*, Mabey's going to fall apart. Mom *has to* come home to visit.

"I can't wait to see her," I say, and I disappear down the hatch.

25

Wednesday Morning

Dad doesn't understand why nobody's talking at breakfast.

Aside from our spoons hitting our bowls, some crunching, and Dad's slurping, it's dead silent at the table this morning. He's reading his tablet as usual, but he keeps looking up at us curiously.

"Quiet today," he notes.

Mabey gives Agnes a death stare, which Agnes ignores.

"Yep," I agree.

Dad waits for Agnes or Mabey to comment. They don't. He shrugs.

"You almost ready?" he asks me.

Dad's driving me to school early today for a meeting of the decorating committee. I don't have to wait for Izzy—she has softball practice this morning. She'll wear her uniform to school, and she has clothes in her locker to change into after that. It's convenient that our extracurricular activities are happening at the same time, but I'm sad we're missing our morning routine. I like having Izzy come by and walk with me to the bus.

I rinse my dishes and put them in the dishwasher, run back upstairs to change my shirt, then meet up with Dad in the hall.

"Be right back," he calls toward the kitchen. "Have a good day, Mabes Babes. Agnes, be ready in twenty minutes, okay?"

Nobody answers.

Dad and I leave, get in the car, and buckle up. "So what's the deal with Agnes and Mabey?" he asks.

Well, Dad, they're mad at each other because Mom said she's coming to visit, and Agnes doesn't believe her, but Mabey does, and I don't know what to think anymore.

"I have no idea."

"Huh." He changes the subject. "How's Sophie?"

Well, Dad, she's about two days away from being busted for stealing money from school, and she plans to blame it on identity theft, which will make it ten times worse.

"She's okay."

"I like Izzy, too," Dad says. "I'm happy to see you making more friends."

I have no *Well, Dad,* for this one.

"Me too."

We move on to other topics: the decorating committee (I tell him I only joined because Sophie asked me to), the dance (I tell him I haven't decided whether to go), and who I might go to the dance with (I tell him it will be a cold day in Satan's backyard when I go to a dance with a date).

"Okay," he says, pulling up to the drop-off. "Have good day, BunBun."

The student council office is closed when I get there, so I go upstairs and put my coat in my locker, play a game on my phone for a few minutes, and then come down the back stairs to see if anybody's there yet. I hear voices coming from the office, and I see the back of Carolina's head as she leans out into the hallway and looks toward the front door. I run up a few stairs and crouch on the landing before she looks in my direction.

"She's not out there," Carolina says to persons unseen. "But with her, you have to check. She's always, like, lurking." She reenters the office and shuts the door behind her.

I don't have to hear a name to know she's talking about me. I'm, like, lurking right now, creeping back down to the first floor and squatting with my ear against the wall. The sound is muffled, but I can still make out the words.

First I hear Desiree's voice. "She's so weird and creepy. The only reason people talk to her is because they need something."

Hannah agrees. "It's sad. It's like, 'What's wrong with you? Why don't you have any real friends?'"

Real friends—ha! Like Hannah's a "real friend" to Carolina. I'd much rather sit alone at lunch than have "real friends" like Hannah, who writes nasty things about the others on the bathroom wall.

Sophie's voice is next. "I know! It's pathetic. She wants to be friends with me so much. She begged to join the decorating committee. I should have told her we didn't need any more help, but... I don't know. I feel sorry for her."

There is giggling and *awwing* over how pitiful I am. I feel light-headed, like all my blood just left my body.

I'm such an idiot.

This is how much of an idiot I am: I thought Sophie really liked me. That's how gullible I am. I thought she and I were becoming actual friends. I helped her out, she gossiped with me, we shared a moment in the resource room... we even met each other's parents, for God's sake! I joined the decorating committee for her!

Now I hear her tell the group that she feels sorry for me. Well, I'm done feeling sorry for her.

The rest of the conversation is drowned out by Rich Savoy, who's laying out some logistics for Will Rasmussen as they come down the back stairs.

"Sophie will have the cash at the Friday lunch meeting," Rich says. "So we can give the DJ a deposit this weekend, and we'll divide the shopping . . ."

I quickly untie and retie my shoe so it doesn't look like I'm crouched there by the bottom step like a goblin for no reason. Rich almost trips on me as they pass. "Oh, hey, Glad."

"Hey."

I straighten up and walk into the office behind Rich and Will. All the girls look at me and then at one another.

I say it loudly enough to be heard by everyone in the room, and even by anyone who might be crouching outside with their ear to the wall: "Hey, I came by to tell you I can't be on the committee anymore. Good luck with the dance."

I turn and walk out of the office, but I can't move fast enough to avoid Carolina's voice—"Um, that was weird."

You know what's even weirder? I think, taking the stairs two at a time in my haste to get away. *You're planning for a dance that's not going to happen.*

26

Wednesday Homeroom

An hour later, my head is still spin-ning from what I overheard.

I want to believe that Sophie didn't mean the things she said about me. Part of me still believes she honestly likes me, and that she was just saying she doesn't for her friends' sake. But when I think about it (which I *cannot* stop doing), it seems pretty obvious that she was telling them the truth and I've been getting the lie. Sophie never paid any attention to me before she needed something; no doubt once she gets what she needs, she'll go back to acting like I don't exist.

Sophie's betrayal isn't the only thing that has

me shook up. Ms. MacDonald is taking attendance, and I'm realizing that Jasmine isn't here. She missed band yesterday, and it looks like she's absent today. It's a little worrisome. But this is probably just a coincidence, right? Jasmine's not . . . missing or something, right?

I don't feel good about this. I don't feel good about anything.

I feel even worse when a teacher's aide comes in with a note for Ms. MacDonald, who peers at it through her glasses and says, "Gladys, Ms. Schellestede needs to speak to you in her office."

There're the obligatory *oooooooh*s as I get up slowly to meet my tragic fate. Someone hums a funeral march; a few people laugh. Ha-ha, guys. This is legit terrifying. And people have literally died of fright—I once read about a seven-year-old boy who was so afraid of the dentist, he had a fatal heart attack in the chair. I drag my feet walking down the hall, thinking about following him to the grave.

Ms. Schellestede is waiting for me with her

office door open. "Come in," she says when I appear. She gestures to one of the chairs in front of her desk but warns me before I sit down, "You'll want to shut the door behind you."

Her door gives the most ominous *creeeeeeeeeeeeeeeeak* as it shuts. It's like the rusty hinges of a dug-up coffin opening to release the undead. I bet she keeps it that way on purpose.

I sit down, and Schellestede fixes me with the Stare, but I'm ready for it. I have a strategy prepared. Look right at her nose, that's what I'm going to do. Just keep my eyes on her nose, and everything will be OH CRAP SHE GOT ME I CAN'T LOOK AWAY. Dang it. The nose was too close to the eyes. Next time I'll go for the forehead.

Her stare drills through my cranium. I don't know what this is about, but I know it's serious. Is it Jasmine? Is she okay? Should I say something? It must be Jasmine. Schellestede must know I gave her the excuses for missing band. That would explain why Gerber came up to me yesterday after school—Schellestede told him I was behind Jasmine's alibis.

Or . . . could this be about Sophie? Maybe Schellestede knows about the money somehow. The student council bought the story about Sophie putting the cash in the bank, but Schellestede is way less gullible. I remind myself that I didn't do anything wrong; I didn't lay a finger on the missing money. I just gave Sophie a story to pass along. Still, I'm starting to sweat.

I wonder if I should rat on Sophie. I feel zero loyalty to her after overhearing her this morning, and maybe I'll get a reduced sentence for giving her up. But what if this is about Jasmine? I don't want to squeal on Sophie—or myself—if she's not the reason I'm here. I don't want to squeal on Jasmine, either, but if she's in some kind of serious trouble, I need to let Schellestede know everything I know. Even though I don't know much.

I'm pretty sure Schellestede can read my thoughts through my eyeballs. If not, she can read them by the panic on my face. The only thing I can do is keep my mouth shut until she tells me what this is about.

Finally, she speaks. "Gladys, I think you know why you're here."

Okay, so she can't actually read my thoughts, or she would have read me trying to answer that exact question. "Honestly, I don't."

Finally, she ends my suspense. "Madison Graham tells me you've been helping people lie again."

Madison. I don't know whether to scream or laugh—I nearly told on myself over Jasmine and Sophie, but it was just Madison! Don't get me wrong, I'm still going to murder her. In fact, I'm going to murder her twice. The worst criminals get multiple life sentences—well, I'm issuing a multiple death sentence on Madison.

I fix my face into an expression of sincere innocence and say what I truly believe: "I didn't do anything wrong."

The Schellestede Stare comes with an add-on

pack: the Eyebrow. Just one, slightly raised. "Madison informed me differently. Apparently, you devised a scheme to pretend you were her boyfriend. And apparently, you're doing the same kind of thing for other students."

Well, I'm stunned. I can't believe Madison told on herself just to get me in trouble. Who even does that? "I didn't—"

Schellestede interrupts me. "You know, Glad, you're very bright. Your grades don't always reflect it, because you're so busy meddling, but I see how smart you are. When Mr. Gerber told me the excuse that Jasmine Gutierrez used for missing band practice, I was impressed. Very sophisticated."

She pauses to see how I react to her accusation. I fight with every muscle of my face to keep my expression neutral while screaming inside.

"Of course," Schellestede continues, "there's no proof that you were part of that lie, and Jasmine denied your involvement when Mr. Gerber spoke to her and her mother last night. She's been suspended for two days. You're lucky you're not being suspended, too."

"But . . ." I falter, terrified by the idea that I could be suspended. If I got suspended from school, Dad would suspend me from a tall building. "I didn't do anything."

"That's not what Madison Graham said." Schellestede deploys both eyebrows this time. "Gladys, I know you mean well. I know you think you're helping people, but you're not. Coming up with lies for other people so they can avoid the consequences of their actions is not helping them."

Mmm . . . I'm not so sure about that. I mean, people specifically ask me to assist them in avoiding consequences, and I do, and they're happy about it. I keep people out of trouble—I'd call that helping them. But I'm not going to interrupt Ms. Schellestede to contradict her.

"You are on thin ice," she says briskly. "I spoke to you about your behavior twice already, and now I've been forced to do it again. If there is a next time, I will call your parents and ask them to join us for this conversation. Have I made myself clear?"

"Yes," I whisper meekly.

Schellestede starts scribbling a late pass for my next class. "All right, then. You can go."

I spring out of my chair like it's an ejector seat. This time, the *creeeeeak* of her door sounds like a prison gate swinging open. And I flee.

27

Wednesday Evening

I am sitting at my desk in my room, crossing names off my list.

It's around sunset, 6:26 p.m. by my clock, and it's quiet in the house. Dad and Mabey aren't home yet, and Baxter and Agnes are downstairs in the kitchen playing dominoes. I played with them for five minutes when I got home, but Agnes kept stopping the game so she could devise a formula to find the probability of picking a double domino from the pile ("If I already have one double, and there's only seven total, then the variable is how many doubles you have, so we'll call that V..."), while Baxter looked at me like, *Please just stand these up in a row and knock them over like a normal child.*

I already checked every app on my phone, watched several videos, and looked up the difference between a llama and an alpaca (llamas can get twice as big and have longer, "banana-shaped" ears). I even did homework for fifteen minutes. Now I need to get serious.

Here's the problem: There is no way for me to get around Ms. Schellestede at school. I know this from working on Harry's case and also from having functioning eyes and ears. I never want to see the inside of Schellestede's office again, and I *definitely* don't want her calling Dad, so . . .

I'm going out of business!

~~*Everything*~~ *Everybody must go! Instead of slashing prices, I'm slashing names!*

~~*Madison*~~ *Done with her.*

~~*Sophie*~~ *SO done with her.*

~~*Harry*~~ *Done with me.*

~~*Jasmine*~~ *Done for.*

Izzy . . .

My pen hovers over the page. I don't want to slash Izzy. She's the only person I'd make an exception for, the only one I don't want to let down. And it's not because I'm lonely and I want her to like me (okay, it's not *just* because I'm lonely and I want her to like me). It's because I honestly like her. And I'm pretty sure she likes me, too. Yesterday as we walked to the bus, she decided my nickname should be "Champ," and everytime she saw me today, no matter who she was with, she yelled, "What's up, Champ!"

Anyway, I think I can afford this one exception. Izzy and I operate outside school hours, so Schell-estede won't find out, and our deal only lasts for two more days.

Izzy stays.

Is that really the end of my list? Usually it's longer, but there's been no new business this past week. I made myself so scarce, people could hardly find me to ask for favors. Taye's been dogging my every move for two days and he still hasn't caught me. Maybe now that Schellestede has shut me down, and I officially can't say yes to anybody's requests, I can start eating lunch in the cafeteria again. Too bad nobody there wants to eat with me. Not even Harry.

My phone chimes with a text from Mabey: need ur help cover 4 me

I want to laugh at the timing. Just as I'm shutting down Glad's Help Desk, Mabey asks for help.

Another few texts come in:

Im gonna b a little late tonight

Tell Dad Nomi's car died

Waiting 4 tow truck or sumthing

I hit her back:

Then I erase the conversation.

It's a good thing Mabey texted when she did, because I hear Dad come through the door and yell hello to Baxter and Agnes. I take a minute before I go downstairs to greet him, so I can imagine the scene I'm about to set. I need to be able to picture it: Mabey and Nomi in Nomi's car (*but Nomi doesn't have her license*), on their way back from some innocent outing (*like what?*), when the car sputters and dies (*in the middle of the road, or were they able to pull over?*).

Mabey didn't give me a lot to work with here.

I leave my room and go downstairs to the kitchen, where Dad has unloaded tonight's takeout: rotisserie chicken with broccoli and mashed potatoes on the side. Agnes is trying to convince Baxter to stay for dinner—"We can play more dominoes!" she enthuses—while Baxter insists he couldn't possibly—"Sorry, I've just got so much, uh, work to catch up on."

"Hey, BunBun," Dad says. He corrals me and kisses my head.

I crack the top off the plastic tub of mashed potatoes and lick the underside. "Hey, DadDad."

"Use a spoon and a plate!" he admonishes, so

I take a plate from the cupboard and a spoon from the drawer. It's always rules, rules, rules with Dad.

Agnes hugs one of Baxter's sequoia-tree legs in an effort to make him stay, but he manages to struggle free, say his goodbyes, and make his exit.

"See you tomorrow, Bax," says Dad. He leans into the hall and calls upstairs: "Mabes Babes! Dinner!"

Okay, that's my cue. Time for me to shine. I say, as casually as I can, "Oh, Mabey called and said she's gonna be late. Nomi's car broke down."

Apparently I did not say it casually enough. Dad stops hacking at the chicken with a greasy knife and looks at me skeptically. "What? Why is she driving around with Nomi? Why didn't she call me instead of calling you?"

Seriously! And why didn't she think of a better story? I put my best spin on it. "Nomi's mom was driving them to look at prom dresses. And she didn't call *me*, she called the home phone. I guess she thought you would be home by now."

Bingo. Dad gets a guilty look on his face. He knows he should have been home an hour ago. We hate it when he works late, and we tell him that all the time. Plus, the mention of prom dresses reminds him that Mabey needs a mom-type person to do mom-type things with, and *our mom isn't here*. Dad wouldn't want Mabey to be deprived of some maternal dress shopping, would he?

It's almost a shame I'm retiring.

When Mabey comes home about a half hour later, Dad and I are watching TV in the living room. "Sorry I'm late." She sighs. "I called and talked to Glad, did she tell you?"

"She did." Dad says. "Thanks. How was dress shopping? Did you see anything you liked for prom?"

Mabey picks up on this cue like the experienced faker she is. "Everything was ugly. And expensive. It's just junior prom, anyway. I'm probably not even going to go." She starts up the stairs toward her room.

"You sure?" asks Dad. "We could go shopping this weekend—"

"UUUUUUGGGHHHH." The sound of her groan trails off as she climbs.

Dad's expression deflates. "Well," he says. "I tried."

"You want me to talk to Mabes?" I offer.

Dad gives me a sad smile. "You're such a good kid, BunBun." Not an answer to my question, but okay. "You're always trying to help out."

The way I glowed all those years ago, when Mom told me about my amazing imagination—that's how I glow from Dad's praise. I'm not as smart as Agnes, but I'm a great helper. I picture Dad walking next to Gloria Nelson at the mall, saying, *Gladdy's such a good kid. She's always trying to help out.*

Do you hear that, Ms. Schellestede?

28

Thursday Morning

Izzy's a no-show this morning.

She's supposed to show up by 7:45 a.m. I text her at 7:50 a.m. to see where she is, but she doesn't text back. I text her a few more times with rising impatience while Dad, Agnes, and Mabey all get ready and leave for the day. I wait for Izzy to show up until the very last minute, but then I have to run for the bus. Izzy's not there at the stop, and she doesn't get on at the stop near her house.

We're pulling up to school when I finally get a text from her: mm at dugout EMERGENCY.

It takes two minutes for me to trot over past the bleachers to the dugout. Hiding in a corner is

Princess Izzy, wearing a peach blouse, a pink skirt, and a frozen grimace of horror. She doesn't even have her cloak to shield her.

"What happened?"

Izzy can barely talk, she's so traumatized. "My grandma drove me to school today. She's leaving on Saturday, so she wants to use every second to tell me how to live my life. I couldn't even text you back, she was in my face the whole time. I tricked her into dropping me off out here, so I don't think anybody saw me, but . . ." She indicates her outfit. "What am I gonna do?"

I'm thinking the same thing: What am I going to do? I can't run to Izzy's locker and get her clothes and come back—once you're in those doors, you don't get to leave until 2:45 p.m. And I can't trade clothes with her—she's two inches taller and more mature than me. Looks like she might have to spend the day hiding in the dugout like a delinquent.

Then I notice the first-aid kit on the wall.

"We're going to have to work with what we've got," I say as I open the kit. "But that means ruining these clothes."

Izzy nods. "Let's do it."

"You're going to get in trouble," I warn her.

"Oh, yeah," she agrees. "But whatever. My grandma's going to have to deal with it sooner or later. I'm done hiding how I look."

"Okay. Let's start with these puffy sleeves." I take the scissors from the kit and start chopping the sleeves off her blouse. It feels like I'm committing a crime, destroying a perfectly good shirt—I have this crazy, reckless feeling that makes me giggle maniacally. Izzy starts giggling, too, but I make her stop so I don't cut either of us accidentally.

I stand back to judge my work. The blouse is still peach, but it's sleeveless and ragged at the edges, so that's an improvement.

"Now the skirt." I kneel before her and cut a six-inch slit up the front, then I do the same to the back. "Adhesive tape," I command, and she hands it to me like a nurse in the operating room. I tape the former skirt to form "shorts," then I bind it to her body with tape and Ace bandages. She looks like a wrestler who couldn't afford real spandex.

"What about the shoes?" she asks. I look down at a pair of pink flats with bows on them. Impossible to fix; must be neutralized.

"What size are you?"

"Five."

"Trade." I take off my sneakers and put on her flats. They clash with my green socks, but whatever, they fit.

"How is it?" Izzy asks. "Still girly? It's the orange shirt, isn't it. Maybe if I rub dirt on it . . . or . . ." She looks around frantically, and her eyes land on the scissors I left on the bench. "I'm going to catch hell for ruining my clothes. Might as well go all the way."

Izzy grabs the scissors and a handful of her hair and hacks off a big chunk right in the front. My mouth falls open.

She grins, swinging one leg over the bench to seat herself. "Here," she says, handing me the scissors. "Take over."

We don't have much time. I start chopping as fast as I can, but these are not hair-cutting scissors. "All the way," she instructs me. "Short as possible."

I give it a few snips, and then we *really* have to go inside. The last thing I want is for Schellestede to see me coming in late with Izzy.

"Now how do I look?" she asks.

Izzy stands before me in a ripped, sleeveless blouse, some bizarre fabric-and-tape garment on her legs, and my sneakers. She looks like she got her head stuck in a fan. "Honestly? Really bad."

"Good."

Heads turn and conversations cease as we walk toward school, but Izzy holds her partially shorn head high. "See ya second period," she says, then peels off to greet her soccer friends, who are pointing and gasping with laughter. "Hey, jackweeds, what's so funny?"

Izzy's outfit keeps them laughing all morning. The teachers are baffled. According to the dress code, her blouse isn't too low-cut, there are no drug or sex references on her garments, and no stomach or underwear is visible. But even after she throws on her soccer shorts (the adhesive tape was failing), she's definitely breaking the "no clothes that are distracting to other students" rule. And she's loving it.

You'd think Schellestede would send a note to Izzy's homeroom and give her a lecture. But Schellestede is not heard from at all. Even as the herd mass-migrates toward the lunchroom, there's no sign of her. Her office door stays closed.

I'm about to skip lunch and go hide somewhere when Izzy grabs me and pulls me into the cafeteria with her. "Glad!" she hoots. "Hey, Champ! Everybody wants an outfit like mine! You gotta come sit with us!"

She starts steering me toward her table, where Taye and Jackson and Liz Kotlinski are assembling. Meanwhile, Sophie's waving at me from her table, wearing a sunny smile. The only clue that everything's not totally fine and normal is the deep crease between her eyebrows. It's like that one part of her face is thirty years older than the rest of her.

Over in the corner, Harry's sitting alone with his sardines. The eighth-grade sharks are circling, and Schellestede's not here to provide even a thin layer of protection.

"I'm gonna sit with Harry," I decide. Even if he doesn't want me to.

"Okay," Izzy says easily, changing direction to stick with me. She yells toward her table, "See you, jackweeds!"

I'm aware of being the center of attention as we head to Harry's table. Izzy's used to it, but I'm not—people turning and looking and whispering to one another. I like to be the observer, not the observed. Meanwhile, Izzy's so happy, I think she might start dressing like this every day.

"Hey," I say, sitting down in the chair across from Harry. Izzy sits next to me.

Harry wants to stay mad at me, but nobody can look at Izzy and be anything but wildly entertained. "Why . . . ?" he begins. Too many questions occur to him at once. "Just why?"

"You don't like it?" Izzy pretends to be wounded. "Glad's the one who did my hair."

Harry cracks an involuntary smile. "It's . . . unique."

"Hey, you're, like, a science person," Izzy realizes. "Do you know about spontaneous combustion? I picked it as my report topic, but I haven't started yet."

"Well, I know it's not real, according to researchers. People don't just blow up while walking down the street . . ."

The three of us go on to have a delightful conversation about arson, tire fires, and how the fat in a human body produces a "candle effect" when burned. People keep coming up to talk to Izzy, and she keeps shooing them away, entranced by Harry's description of what happens when you get hit by lightning. "So, wait, your shoes literally get blown apart from the steam of your body? And your watch gets superheated and melts into your arm?"

"Basically, anything metal on your body . . ."

I notice that Declan the burnout keeps walking by our table, waiting for us to leave so he can harass Harry. When he circles back for a third pass, Izzy stands up and blocks his path. Her ragged spikes of hair and the expression on her face make her look like a postapocalyptic warrior queen. "What do you want, jackweed?"

"Nothing," says Declan, moving on.

"That's right." Izzy sits down again and picks up the conversation with Harry. "Anyway, so anything metal on your body is going to melt?"

"Yep. Even the rivets on your jeans."

Izzy's jaw hangs open. "They actually, like, super-melt through your skin?"

Speaking of super-melt, I feel two sizzling spots on my back. When I turn around, Schellestede is standing there, arms folded. She looks at Izzy, noting the hacked-off hair and the ripped, dirty blouse. Then she turns to me, noting the incredibly busted look on my face. Obviously, there's something fishy going on here. Obviously, I am involved.

"So, ladies." Schellestede gives us her iciest smile and pins us both with the Stare. "Why don't the two of you come to my office and explain what's going on here."

29

Thursday After School

I am walking toward my doom.

Actually, I'm walking toward my bus. But since the bus will bring me home, and Dad texted to say that he'll be there to discuss the call he received from Ms. Schellestede today, it's basically the same thing.

In working on my own case, I've come up with several key points I want to emphasize:

1. I didn't do anything wrong.
2. None of this was my idea.
3. People asked me to help them.
4. Didn't Dad tell me last night that I'm a good kid for trying to help people?

5. All I did was text one girl and cut another girl's hair!
6. What's so terrible about that?
7. It's not like anybody got hurt! Everything is fine!
8. Why is everybody making such a big deal out of this?
9. Yes, Dad, I do understand the epic lecture you've just given me about rules, laws, and the social contract between all citizens. In the future, I will consider the consequences of my actions and will refrain from violating any more *stupid, nonexistent* school rules about *I don't even know what, because* . . .
10. I didn't do anything wrong!

This should go well.

Strangely, when I pass by Madison and her friends, she looks nervous. No victorious smirk today, even though she must know that I was just in Schellestede's office, for the second day in a row, where I was sentenced to detention for a week. Madison won, I lost. You'd think she'd be jumping for joy.

Then I remembered what Izzy said: *They're scared of you.* No wonder Madison looks terrified. She knows it was a bad move to tell on me. Now that I'm out of the fixing game, I don't need to keep people's secrets. There's no more "I know nothing, I remember nothing, and I delete everything" guarantee. I could go up to her friends right now and tell them the true story of James the Dead Canadian Boyfriend.

Actually . . . I *do* have a minute before I need to board the bus. I change course and veer toward their cluster. Now I'm the one with the victorious smirk.

Madison's two closest friends, Violet and Vanessa, have their backs to me, so they don't see me approach. "We knew he was fake the whole time," Violet is saying to Madison.

Vanessa laughs. "I mean, do you think we're that stupid, that we would believe you? That's hilarious." She and Violet shake their heads, incredulous.

Violet puts on a concerned voice. "You know, you need professional help. It's not funny anymore. You're seriously warped."

Vanessa just sounds disgusted. "Like, at least get meds or something."

Madison stares at the ground like she's shutting everything out. She seems to have plenty of practice at it. I never paid that much attention to their little group, but now that I think about it, Violet and Vanessa do kind of kick Madison around a lot. Sometimes at lunch I'll see Madison sitting alone, in exile from their table; then the next day, they're all sitting together again. I would rather have no friends than friends like that.

No wonder Madison wants to live in a fantasy world.

I didn't used to have an opinion on Violet and

Vanessa, but from right now until forever I HATE THEM. *I* was supposed to be the one making Madison feel like crap, but they got there first. And now they're actually making me *feel sympathy for Madison*. Madison! Who got me in trouble! On purpose! It is *so unfair* that I am feeling sorry for her at this moment, and it's all their fault.

I turn away without interrupting them, grumbling the whole time. Too late, I see Sophie in pursuit.

"Hey, Glad!"

Sophie plants herself in front of me and gives me an air-kiss. She seems all bubbly and peppy, as usual, but close up, I can see that her teeth are clenched behind her smile and the veins in her temples are bulging. "So-oo," she begins, wrinkling her nose adorably.

"What. Do. You. Want."

Sophie's eyes widen with alarm at my unfriendly tone. She keeps up her happy face, but she drops her voice to a low murmur. "Glad, I don't know what to do. They want the money tomorrow."

If I had a smile left inside me, I'd be wearing it right now. "I know. I heard Rich mention it before the meeting yesterday morning. Right after I heard you tell all the girls how pathetic I am."

Sophie's eyes widen. She stumbles back a step and clasps both hands over her mouth. "Oh my God," she says, voice trembling. "No, Glad, that was . . . I'm so sorry. I only said that . . . I didn't want them to know . . ."

"Oh!" I interrupt. "The part about me begging to join the committee, that was a nice touch. Good detail."

If Sophie gets any paler, she will become translucent. "Honestly, I swear I didn't mean it. I don't feel that way, I swear, please, I was just trying to cover—"

"Cover up the real reason you'd be talking to me, I know. Because people only talk to me when they need something. Isn't that what Hannah said? Or was it Desiree . . ."

"It's not true." There are tears in Sophie's eyes.

I wonder if anyone is looking. Then I wonder why I wondered that, because who cares if people are looking? It's not my problem anymore. "Glad, please, I do like you, I swear. Please believe me. Please, Glad. I need help."

Nope. Not this time. I fell for this once already, during our conversation in the resource room. I'm not even wobbling for it now. Sophie needs help? We all need help. I'm in severe trouble right now, both at home and at school, and nobody's doing a heckin' thing to help me.

"Sorry." *Not sorry*, I add silently as I brush past her. "I've got my own problems."

30

Thursday Afternoon

I'm in the living room, getting lectured for the second time today.

Dad's been at it for a while already, emphatically repeating his own list of key points:

1. Rules are rules!
2. They're not optional!
3. Did you think you could break a rule without consequences?
4. Do you think you're above rules somehow?
5. You were warned twice not to do something and you did it a third time!

6. Nobody's going to trust you to follow the rules now!

7. The exact rule you broke? "Don't do whatever Ms. Schellestede said not to do!"

8. BECAUSE SHE SAID NOT TO DO IT.

9. Okay, you are right: people blindly followed orders in Nazi Germany, and that was wrong. But you are not in Nazi Germany, you are in the seventh grade and are simply being asked to stop concentrating on other people's problems and keep your eyes on your own damn work!

10. Why do you keep doing this?

Dad was on number five when Baxter dropped Agnes off and discreetly left. Agnes either went downstairs to her lab or pretended to go downstairs to her lab, in which case she's listening very quietly from the kitchen. Now he's on the big one, point number ten: *Why?*

"What is so rewarding about this..." Dad searches for the words as he paces the living room. "This liar-for-hire thing you do?"

"I don't lie," I insist (though "liar-for-hire" does sound kind of cool). "I do favors for people."

Dad's face clearly shows that he is not having any of this, not even a tiny little slice. "Favors like helping a girl lie about her whereabouts when she's supposed to be at band practice?"

Damn it, Jasmine. Why'd you have to get caught? "Why does everyone keep accusing me of that?"

Dad is not going to fall for the old "answering a question with a question" trick. "Then tell me what favors you mean."

"Well...," I stall, trying to think which jobs sound the most innocent. "Like, this one guy Taye wanted me to give a box of chocolates to his crush."

"Okay," Dad says, unconvinced.

"And... this guy Sam Boyd was going to get

238

beat up by this girl Evelyn Ferszt, so I wrote him a letter to give to her. And she didn't beat him up!"

"Okay. And what about Izzy, whose hair you chopped off with scissors? Was that a favor for her?"

"Yes! She asked me to cut her hair!"

I'd like to note that Izzy repeatedly made this point very clear in our meeting with Schellestede: "I asked Glad to do it. She didn't do anything wrong. Glad didn't break the dress code, I did."

This made no difference whatsoever, but it was appreciated.

"And her coming over in the morning to walk to the bus? Was that friendship, or a favor?"

I look at him sheepishly. "Her grandma made her wear girl stuff to school this week. So she came over to change clothes."

"Oh." Dad is audibly disappointed. He was so happy to see me making friends. "And Sophie? I assume our shopping trip was some kind of business."

"Yeah."

"Oh. Huh."

Dad falls silent, but he's not giving me the Lawyer Look. He's not looking at me at all. He's staring at the wall in front of him like he's trying to read a very small sign. I sit and wait for him to say something.

After a minute or two, he asks, "Why do you do it?"

I don't know anymore. It doesn't matter anyway. I already decided I was going to stop—I *have* stopped, but this morning Izzy needed me. "Because . . . I like helping people."

Dad's expression softens. "I know you like helping people, BunBun. That's one of the best things about you. I don't want you to think you shouldn't help people, because you should. We all should. Everybody needs help sometimes. But sometimes we think we're helping someone, and we're not."

This is the same thing Schellestede tried to tell

me. *I know you think you're helping people* . . . I'm so frustrated I want to cry.

Dad continues. "If a classmate of yours skips band and you help her get away with it, you're not helping her. You're just making it easier for her to keep skipping band. If she doesn't want to go to practice, she should quit, but she shouldn't be lying about her whereabouts. That's unsafe. Nobody knew where she was or who she was with. What if something had happened to her? Do you see what I'm saying?"

I nod, sneaking a look at the time display on the cable box. We've been at this for over an hour—surely we must be done here. I risk asking, "Can I go now?"

"No," says Dad. He stands in front of me, scrutinizing my face. "Now I want to know what kind of 'fixing' you're doing here at home."

Okay. I was *not* prepared for this. A bead of sweat trickles down my back. "I'm not doing anything," I answer.

There's an extended silence from Dad. He tips his head and stares at me. Lawyer Look in full effect. "I find that hard to believe," he says finally.

"It's true." I fold my arms and sulk at Dad's mistrust. "I'm not 'fixing' anything at home."

"Look at me," he demands. I lift my head unwillingly. "What about last night, when Mabey was late? Did you come up with her excuse?"

Eeep, says my brain.

"No," I croak.

(*Yes, totally*, says my facial expression. Fortunately, facial expressions are not admissible evidence in court.)

Dad sits and looks at me in silence. I look back at him until I can't stand it anymore, then I look away. What does he want me to say? I didn't do anything wrong. *I'm* not the one who came home late last night with a cheap excuse, so why doesn't he go yell at Mabey? Hasn't he yelled at me enough today? Especially after Schellestede already yelled at me? Haven't I had enough of people yelling at me today?

I'm so mad right now. I'm always stuck in the middle. Whether it's Dad against Mabey, or Mom against Dad, or Mabey against Agnes, or Agnes against Mom, every fight is the same. The earth quakes, and the ground underneath me cracks, leaving Mabey and Mom on one side and Agnes and Dad on the other. And I fall into the giant crevasse between them, bouncing off rocks on my way down, until I drown in the boiling lava of Earth's core.

I bring my fist down on the couch cushion next to me. "I'm not fixing anything at home!" I yell. "Because there's nothing in this house that can be fixed! This whole family is broken!"

I hurl myself off the couch, past Dad and his stupid shocked face, and up the stairs to my room.

31

Friday Morning

I don't know what's up with Mabey today.

I'm the one in trouble with Dad. *I'm* the one with detention for the next week. And *I'm* the one who covered for her the other night, so she wouldn't get busted for being late. So I can't imagine why *she's* the one stomping around her room, slamming the bathroom door, and growling at me when I knock.

I use Dad's bathroom instead, then get dressed and go downstairs for breakfast, exchanging good mornings with Dad and Agnes. Dad seems slightly less mad at me today, or maybe he's just distracted by Agnes, who's in the middle of telling him about a new math term she learned.

"Zepto," she explains, "is a prefix meaning 'ten to the negative twenty-first power.'"

"Oh, that's handy," says Dad, before taking a big *sluuuuuurp* of coffee. "Now I can stop saying 'ten to the negative twenty-first power' all the time, and just say 'zepto.'"

His phone rings, and he rises from his seat as he answers. "Hey, Baxter. What's up . . . Oh, sorry to hear it . . ."

Mabey clomps into the kitchen, grabs a glass and plate for herself, puts an English muffin in the toaster, and slumps into her seat at the table. She's wearing the same sweatshirt she slept in, her hair is up in a sloppy bun, and it's kind of obvious that she didn't shower.

Dad ends his call and joins us at the table. "Well, Baxter is sick, and I have an appointment after work tonight. So, Mabes, I need you to pick up Agnes from school and walk home with her."

"Why do I have to do it?" she whines.

"I'll do it," I offer.

"You have detention," Dad reminds me sternly. Oh, right.

"I can walk home by myself," Agnes suggests.

"No, you can't." Dad shuts this right down. He's a little overprotective. Mom used to let me and Mabey walk places when we were Agnes's age, but Dad reads way too many news stories about missing kids, and he doesn't feel comfortable letting a nine-year-old walk through our totally safe, boring suburb, especially on the busier roads. "That's a forty-five-minute walk, at least. I'd like you to be accompanied."

"Why can't you do it?" Mabey complains.

"I have a meeting." He turns to me. "With Gloria Nelson, in fact."

I nearly spit-spray my juice all over the table.

Dad continues. "Sophie's consulting idea got Gloria thinking about starting her own business. She has a few questions about incorporating. So we're going to grab a quick bite. I'll be home by eight thirty at the latest."

A meeting? A quick bite? Well, at least he's not all dressed up and singing, like it's a date. Because he might be home a lot sooner than he thinks. Today is deadline day for Sophie—she's supposed to hand over the cash at lunch. If it doesn't go well, she might need her mom pretty badly. She might even need a lawyer.

I feel a little ill at the prospect of Sophie's downfall. It triggers me into Fixing Mode before I even realize what I'm doing. Maybe I could go with Sophie when she confesses to the council? Or . . . maybe Harry could help somehow! That's a great idea. Why didn't I think to ask him sooner? I bet he could think of something . . .

The stern, internal voice of reason interrupts me. *NO HELPING*, it says. *And especially NO HELPING SOPHIE.*

Right. We already did that, and she sold us out. Sorry, Sophie, but you're on your own.

I say bye, take off, and walk to the bus stop alone. I'm glad Izzy's not hiding how she dresses anymore, but selfishly I wouldn't mind if she still had a reason to come over and change and walk to the bus with me. I wonder how it went for her after school yesterday. If I got lectured and grounded and had my phone taken away, I can only imagine what kind of punishment Izzy got when she came home looking like she got in a fight with a lawn mower.

I board the bus and take a third-row seat. When Izzy gets on one stop later, she's wearing jeans, a T-shirt, a baseball cap, and a huge grin. She stops dramatically at the front of the aisle, whips off the hat, and the whole bus goes nuts.

Izzy is bald.

Not all the way bald, but close—there's less than a centimeter of fuzz on her scalp. She dips her buzz-cut head as she starts down the aisle so people can rub it. When she gets to me, she stops and sits for a minute. "Hey, jackweed. Sorry I ruined your work."

"How'd it go?"

"Well, Grandma flipped out, so there was a couple hours of her yelling at me. My dad's punishing me until she leaves. And Ashley made me swear I'd get some new clothes." She sees my dismay and laughs. "Not different-style clothes. Just, like, *new* jeans and T-shirts."

"So . . . everything's okay?"

"Well, I mean, Grandma's cutting me out of her will. And I'm probably not getting a birthday card with twenty dollars in it this year. She's *super*-mad at my dad—it's a good thing she leaves tomorrow." She runs a hand over her fuzzy head and grins. "Anyway. I'm sorry you got in trouble for helping me. What'd your dad say?"

I condense the three-hour lecture for her. "He's taking my phone away for the weekend."

"Oh. That sucks." Izzy rises again so she can join her pals in the back-of-the-bus squad. "Are you gonna go to the dance next Saturday?"

"I don't think so."

"What? You gotta come!" She slugs me in the arm and continues down the aisle so the rest of her jackweed friends can feel her head. "Later, Champ."

I don't see Sophie outside before school. I guess she got smart and decided to be absent today—that'll give her until Monday to see if she can raise the money somehow. But then I see her going into second-period English, pretending to smile, looking like she's going to pass out any second. Desiree and Hannah are chatting with her, oblivious to her distress, and I realize that I am the only person in the world who knows what she's going through right now.

I can't seem to stop looking over at her, as the class reviews apostrophes and when to use them. Mr. Cruea reminds us that you use an apostrophe and the letter *s* to indicate possession (e.g., This is Sophie*'s* problem). You also use an apostrophe *s* to contract the word *is* (e.g., Sophie*'s* in a world of trouble).

Once again, I'm too good at what I do. A light blinks on, and the words start coming to me. Fifteen minutes later, when class is nearly over, and Mr. Cruea is ready to rip out his own hair in frustration because Olivia Kurtzweil keeps asking if apostrophes make words plural, I have come up with the perfect story for Sophie to give the council.

The truth.

Dear Student Council Members,
I made a very bad mistake and I regret it. I have no excuses. I made the wrong choice, I lied about it, and I have to tell the truth now. For the past year, I've had a problem I've tried to hide. I take things that aren't mine. I could tell you all the reasons I've told myself to explain why I did it, but I won't. I'll just tell the truth. I took the money for the dance. I am so sorry for betraying your trust. I will repay every dime as soon as I can, and I will accept whatever consequences I've earned with my behavior. I'm very, very sorry for letting you down.

I catch up to her in the hall after class. "Hey, Sophie."

"Hey." She's startled that I'm talking to her, but she hangs back from Hannah and Desiree to hear what I have to say. We step into a corner and I give her the note.

Sophie holds her breath and her eyes fill with tears as she reads it. When she's done, she presses it to her chest, closes her eyes, and exhales heavily. It looks like she's saying a silent prayer.

"I thought they might go easier on you if they understand why you did it," I tell her.

Sophie opens her teary eyes and looks at me with pure gratitude. "I can't believe you did this for me."

Yeah, well. I can't fully believe it, either. "I wanted to help."

"You *did* help," Sophie insists. "You have no idea, Glad. I couldn't have gotten through these last two weeks without you. I never told anybody about my . . . taking things. But you knew the truth about me and you still stuck by me. That's the only thing that's been giving me hope. If you could accept me, maybe other people can, too." She dabs at her eyes with the back of one wrist. "I never should have said we weren't friends. You've been such a good friend to me."

The second bell is about to ring. Hannah calls to Sophie from down the hallway, "Come on, witch!"

Sophie takes my hand and squeezes it in hers. "Will you come with me? When I tell the council? I don't think I can do it alone."

Desiree and Hannah are watching closely now. Is Sophie Nelson actually holding my cootie-covered hand? On purpose? It's just because she feels sorry for me, though. Right?

"I'll meet you in the hall by the caf," I say. "We'll do this together."

"Thanks." One more squeeze before she drops my hand and rushes off to catch up with her girls. Then she turns and calls to me down the busy hallway, for everybody to hear: "Glad! You're an awesome friend!"

Two periods later, I'm on my way to meet Sophie when Taye catches me in the hall and falls in step beside me. "Hey," he says. "I'm really sorry about . . . what I said the other day."

You mean when you called me a freak? I'm sorry you said that, too.

"I got nervous that people were watching. The second I said it, I wanted to take it back. I'm really sorry, Glad."

Whatever. I get that he's sorry, and I'm happy he said so. But it hurt me. Like, a lot. Even now, a few days later, I don't know if I'm ready to say *That's okay.* Instead I go with "Thanks."

Taye stays next to me down the stairs, until I stop on the first floor, and he stops, too. He puts one hand around the back of his neck like he's trying to cover a sunburn. Actually, he does look a little red. "So . . . listen," he says.

I'm listening, and what I hear is a request

coming. I shake my head no and cut him off. "I'm not going to carry another package."

He looks dejected, but he nods. He must have expected my response. "Thanks anyway," he says. "Sorry again."

One nice thing: Since I no longer care about pleasing my clients, I can say whatever I want. "Taye, anonymous gifts are getting you nowhere. Just deliver the message yourself!" I tell him. "It's the only way you're going to get a response."

"But . . ." I watch him struggle with this idea, weighing the risk against the reward. What if Taye bares his heart to the Target and gets humiliated? But then again, the Target might be super-happy and excited to be liked by Taye. Maybe they could be a thing.

"Okay," Taye decides. He takes a huge breath in and out for courage. "You're right. I'm going to tell him tonight. You really are the best, Glad."

Okay. One day I might forgive him after all.

I'm still waiting for Sophie, who's probably (a) puking in the bathroom or (b) running away from the building right now. Everyone else has gone in to lunch when the door to Schellestede's office *creeeeeeaks* open, and Jasmine and her mom emerge. Jasmine's mom, a stout woman in makeup and workout clothes, looks mighty pissed, holding Jasmine by the upper arm like she's a seven-year-old about to get a spanking. But Jasmine appears perfectly content, with a dreamy expression on her placid face.

"Jasmine!" I'm so relieved to see her, I practically weep. I rush over and embrace her, breaking her mom's grasp. "Where've you been?" I whisper. "I was worried."

"I said you didn't help me," she whispers back. "I wouldn't snitch on you."

"I know. I was worried about *you*."

"We're leaving right now," Jasmine's mom growls, retaking her daughter's arm to haul her out of school, perhaps even out of existence. I manage to get in a few last words before she's dragged away.

"What happened? Are you okay?"

Jasmine flashes a huge smile over her shoulder at me. "I'm great!" she calls. "I have a boyfriend!"

"NO, YOU DO NOT!" Her mom's voice echoes in the hall as they disappear.

When I turn around, Sophie's right next to me, her confession folded in her hand. She looks shaky and pale, but there're no chunks on her shoes or anything, so I guess she kept breakfast down. "Okay," she says, determined. "Here goes."

Sophie keeps her head high as we walk over to the A+ table, where Rich Savoy is getting ready to start the meeting. "Great, here's Sophie. Is everyone else here? Where's Carolina?" He looks surprised at seeing me. "Oh, hey, Glad. Are you . . . rejoining us?"

Sophie makes my answer unnecessary. "Rich? Before we start, I have to say something."

Everybody at the table turns their attention to Sophie. Her hands tremble as she unfolds the note. I feel like fainting.

"'I made a very bad mistake,'" Sophie begins, her voice shaking. "'And I regret it. I have no excuses...'"

"*Yeah*, you made a mistake." From out of no-where, Carolina swoops over to the table and hands Sophie a fat envelope. "You dropped this in the hall, dummy."

Sophie blinks a few times, looking at the envelope in her hands like she's never seen such a thing before. What is this rectangular pocket made of paper? And what's inside—grayish-green papers with numbers on them? Is it...money? Could it be...$450?

CLUNK.

Jaw, meet floor.

Sophie hands the envelope to Rich, obviously dazed. I can barely believe it myself. Carolina knew about the missing money? How? Since when? And how was she able to raise that kind of cash so quickly?

Carolina smiles. "You're lucky I was behind you."

I don't like to give her any credit, but yeah. Sophie is very lucky to have Carolina behind her. I still have many, many bad things to say about Carolina Figgis, but I'll never say she's a fake friend to Sophie.

"That's great, Carolina," Rich Savoy says, with just a hint of suspicion. "But, Sophie, what were you going to say?"

Sophie has not yet recovered from her shock. She looks at me, mouth hanging open. The note I wrote is still in her hand, damp with sweat and bleeding ink on her palms. I can practically hear her thinking, *What do I do now?*

I shrug and give her a sad smile. I can't help her anymore. She's got to help herself.

Sophie nods, returns the sad smile, and begins to read again. "'I made a very bad mistake and I regret it. I have no excuses. I made the wrong choice, I lied about it, and I have to tell the truth now.'"

I see facial expressions change as Sophie makes her confession. "'For the past year, I've had a problem I've tried to hide . . .'"

Carolina looks devastated, Rich looks concerned, Hannah looks positively overjoyed. There's going to be an open seat on the student council and an open seat at the head of their lunch table, and Hannah has her eye on both.

Carolina stands next to Sophie, taking her hand and squeezing it. Sophie squeezes back. They're both crying, but she keeps reading. "'I . . . I take things that aren't mine . . .'"

I don't need to hear the rest of it, because I wrote it. And I can already see Rich's stern expression softening in sympathy—I know the council will deal with her fairly. They have the money; there's no need to press any charges. This will be the end of Sophie's student council career, but it won't be the end of her life.

I slip away from the table to go join Izzy and Harry at ours, grinning as I approach. And I sit down right where I belong.

"Hey, jackweeds."

32

Friday After School

Detention wasn't so bad.

All you have to do is sit there for forty-five minutes. I'm very good at sitting. It was way worse for Izzy, because she was missing softball practice—she kept looking longingly out the window in the direction of the ball field. After we were dismissed, we walked over to the field together, she caught the last fifteen minutes of practice with the team, and then we all got on the late bus, which serves both the kids with extracurricular activities and the delinquents with detention like me.

Nobody's there when I get home. That's weird. Mabey should have picked up Agnes and brought her home by now, but there's no stuff in the hall-way, no voices shouting hi. I yell for Mabey and get no answer; I go up to the attic, but it's empty.

On my way downstairs to the lab, I call Agnes's flip phone, the relic Dad makes her carry for emergencies. Her phone, sitting on her lab table, buzzes mockingly at me.

Okay! No problem. I'm sure Mabey picked up Agnes, and they decided to stop off on the walk home and get some food or something. Nothing to worry about. They'll be here any minute. They're simply enjoying a delicious order of French-fried potatoes at a fast food restaurant, and that's taken them . . . I check the time . . . an hour and a half.

I think I'll text Mabey.

Where r u and Agnes? Nobody's home.

I look around the lab while I wait for a reply, as though Agnes is hiding somewhere, or I might find clues to her whereabouts. My phone rings—it's Mabey.

"I FORGOT!" she yells. "I forgot I had to pick

up Agnes today, oh my God! She's not there? What am I going to do?"

Instantly, I panic. What is Mabey going to do? What am *I* going to do? Most important, what is *Agnes* going to do? Her school got out an hour and a half ago—has she been waiting there in front the whole time? Maybe she called Dad to pick her up . . . No, she doesn't have her phone. But maybe a teacher saw her waiting outside and called Dad? That's probably what happened. Agnes is probably somewhere safe with Dad right now.

Unless she decided to walk home alone. In which case, she should have been here forty-five minutes ago.

Mabey's still shrieking in my ear. "You have to cover for me. Say I got sick at school, and . . . and . . . I don't know! Think of something!"

I'm thinking of many things. Calling the school. Calling Dad. Jumping on my bike and searching for Agnes along the route she'd take if she were walk-ing home. My brain has gone into frantic Fixing

Mode, but coming up with an excuse for Mabey is not on its to-do list.

"I'm coming home right now," she says. "We'll find Agnes. Don't tell Dad!"

She hangs up. I take a minute to calm down and clear my head. I don't want to jump to any conclusions—just because Agnes isn't here doesn't mean she's in trouble. She might still be waiting at school.

I look up the school's number and call, my voice shaking along with my hands. I'm surprised the man I'm talking to can understand me. "Um, I'm Gladys Burke . . . calling because she, um, my sister . . . Agnes . . . is she there?"

She is not. According to the nice man, she left at the end of the day with everyone else. I stutter a thank-you and hang up.

So Agnes is not at school. Beloved Agnes the Genius, the world's greatest student, everybody's favorite daughter, is not at school. Okay. My nervous system is hopping all over the place, yelling,

AGNES IS MISSING! DO SOMETHING! But my slightly less-nervous system is telling me to calm down.

I don't want to be like Dad. I don't want to freak out and assume the worst when one little thing is awry. I'm sure Agnes is fine. Here's what probably happened: When Mabey didn't show up, Agnes asked someone to use their phone and called Dad, then he came and got her, and she's at his office right now, playing Sudoku. I'll just text Dad to confirm.

Is Agnes with you?

No reply.

Right, then. I'll assume they're at the office. But just in case, I think I'll go get my bike. Agnes is fine, I know it, but I might as well take a long, healthy ride on this sunny afternoon. And I might as well take it in the direction of Agnes's school.

I'm in the garage grabbing my bike and helmet when my phone rings. Dad.

"No, Agnes is not with me," he fumes. "I just

got out of a meeting, and I'm on my way to meet Gloria Nelson. Agnes is supposed to be home with Mabey. They're not there?"

How do I answer this without getting Mabey in trouble? "Not yet," I say brightly. "But I'm sure they're on the way."

"Well, then call Agnes," he commands, like I didn't do that right away. "And text Mabes and find out where they are. Let me know as soon as you do." He ends the call.

Mabey comes bursting in through the front door, out of breath, and drops her bag where she stands. "Is she here? Is she here?" I shake my head, and she wails, "Oh my God! What am I gonna do?"

Mabey starts fanning herself with both hands like she's going to pass out. "Okay," she says, thinking out loud. "Um, um, um . . . okay. I was, like, five minutes late picking up Agnes, so she decided to walk home, so she wasn't at school when I got there. And . . . I didn't call Dad right away because . . . I figured she just left and I'd catch up to her . . ." Her voice trails off and she looks at me desperately. "You have to help me!"

No, actually, I don't. I don't *have* to help anybody. What a revelation! "Why? This is your fault!"

"It was a mistake!" she wailed. "Mistakes happen!"

Yeah, that's what Mom used to say when she blew things off. That's what Sophie said when she was still lying to herself. *Mistakes happen.* Except . . . they don't. The dance money didn't steal and spend itself. Lies don't tell themselves. Mistakes don't happen unless we make them happen. And they don't stop until we admit: *I made this mistake.*

"I'm calling Dad," I decide.

Mabey bursts into tears. "You can't! He'll kill me!"

True. Also, beside the point right now. "I don't care! Agnes is missing!"

"She's not missing!" Mabey screeches. Her self-fanning has devolved into random flailing. "We just don't know where she is!"

I hope she smacks herself in the head, so I don't have to do it for her. "That's what 'missing' means!"

I press Dad's number on my phone. Mabey turns from me and scurries upstairs to her room, letting the hatch bang shut behind her.

Dad picks up right away, like he's been waiting for my call. "Are they back yet?"

"No," I say, as calmly as I can. "Mabey's here, but Agnes isn't."

"What?" His tone goes from slightly irked to massively annoyed. "Where's Agnes?"

"We . . ." My words get stuck in my throat. I've broken bad news many times before, but this is different. "We don't know."

"What? What are you talking about?"

"Mabey forgot to pick her up, and Agnes left her phone at home. I called the school and they said she left a while ago."

I listen to Dad's loud, angry breathing as he thinks for a second. "I'm getting in the car, and I'm going to drive around until I find her. You and

Mabey stay right there—don't go anywhere. And call me right away if she comes in."

He hangs up. I don't know what to do with myself. I still want to bike around to look for Agnes, but Dad said stay here, and today is not a good day to disobey him. What else can I do? How else can I help? I can't just stand here in the kitchen, powerless to make the situation better.

I think I'll go stand in the attic, powerless to make the situation better.

I climb up to Mabey's room and push my way in. She's on her bed with her face mooshed into a pillow. Her body is still hitching with little sobs.

"Dad's going to look for her in the car," I report.

Mabey keeps her face buried and says nothing, aside from a few hitches. Is she angry at me? Because that would be ridiculous. *I'm* not the one who lost Agnes. *I'm* the one trying to fix things. "I had to call him. You know that, right?"

She stays facedown and silent. I shove her

shoulder to make her move. "Come on. We should go downstairs and wait."

Still nothing. I shove her a few more times, annoyed. "Come on," I prod. "Don't make me do this alone."

Mabey finally lifts her face from the pillow. She doesn't look mad at me. She looks anguished and racked with guilt. "If anything happens to Agnes...," she says, breaking down and sobbing again. "It's all my fault."

Great. Now I feel bad for Mabey.

I try to reassure her. "Nothing's going to happen, and it's not all your fault. Agnes is okay. Dad will drive around and find her, or she'll come walking in any minute. She's smart—she's not going to, like, get in a car with a stranger. It's just taking her a while to get home."

Mabey nods gratefully. She sits up into a cross-legged position and tries to control her runny snot situation with her sleeve. "I'm so stupid," she says, hanging her head. "I can't believe how stupid I am."

Her left forearm is quickly soaked, so she switches to her right one, holding her forearm under her nose, which continues to drip. It would probably work better if she stopped crying. "You didn't do it on purpose," I say.

"Not that." Mabey looks up at me tentatively. "I talked to Mom last night. She's not coming."

Oh.

Of course.

I feel like I've been punched in the stomach. I'm so upset, it's hard to breathe. I'm so disappointed, and so mad at her, and SO mad at myself. What was I thinking? How stupid am I? How gullible can a person be? Of course Mom's not coming. Of course. Why would she act differently than she's acted for most of my life? This is what Mom does: Mom breaks promises. Mom makes excuses. Mom doesn't show up.

I didn't think this afternoon could get any worse, so, *Thanks, Mom, for the opposite of help*. My face is hot, I still haven't caught my breath, and

I want to destroy something—smash it on the floor, break it, and jump up and down on the pieces until they're dust. All the plans I made for her visit, all the work I did, all the hopes I had, have all gone down the drain.

Mabey bursts into a fresh round of tears and brings her fist down on the mattress next to her. "Why did she say she was going to visit? Why does she always do this?"

I know what I should say here: *She didn't do it on purpose.* Or *You know she misses us.* I should fix this situation—make excuses for Mom, tell Mabey what she wants to hear, get her to calm down so we can focus on Agnes.

But all I can think about is that day, years ago, when Mom did this exact same thing: forgot where she was supposed to be and left Agnes waiting after school. I'm remembering how Mom got me to lie for her, to tell Agnes it was all a dream and make her doubt reality. I can't believe I did that to my sister. I can't believe Mom did that to her daughter.

I swear to God, the minute Agnes walks safely through the door, I'm telling her the truth about that day.

Mabey keeps crying, but my eyes have dried. "I don't know why Mom does anything," I say.

And I'm done trying to figure it out. I'm done trying to make Mom come home. I'm done watching what I say to her, and I no longer care about pushing too hard or upsetting her. I'm not making any more lists of things she likes. I'm not going to call the farm over and over and listen to that busy signal. I'm done with "the timing." And I am extra-finally-finished trying to change Dad, or myself, or my sisters, so Mom will love us more.

I no longer care about Mom coming home. All I care about is Agnes coming home. "I'm going downstairs in case Agnes comes in," I say, going for the hatch.

Mabey wipes her eyes and clears her throat. "I'll be right there."

I'm coming down the stairs when Dad's car

screeches into the driveway. He bursts through the door, alone, and sees me there in the hall. "She's still not here?"

"No."

"Damn it." Not the answer he wanted. He starts pacing around the hall, into the kitchen, back into the hall. "I didn't see her anywhere. I drove back and forth three times, different routes . . . I don't know what to do next. Do I keep looking? I don't want to call the police if it's not an emergency . . ."

I don't think I've ever seen Dad without an answer. It's one of Mom's biggest complaints: *Your father has all the answers*. Like that's a bad thing! Personally, I'd love it right now if Dad were being a know-it-all, saying I should calm down and assess the situation, telling me what to do, instead of pacing around and muttering.

"I'm *extremely* angry at your sister," he fumes, and I cringe for Mabey. "She should *not* have left her phone at home, and she should *not* have left school.

She should have stayed and waited, then had the school call me."

Wait. He's not talking about Mabey. He's mad at Agnes. Has Dad ever been mad at Agnes before?

Mabey appears at the top of the stairs. "I'm sorry, I'm so sorry. I swear, it was an accident—"

Dad cuts her off. "Do you see how upset I am right now?" He points to his face: exhibit A. "This is why I want you to call when you're going to be late! Do you understand? Because I worry about you! I'm not trying to run your life! I don't want to ruin your fun! I need you to call so I know where you are!"

"I'm sorry, I'm sorry," Mabey babbles, weeping. "Dad, I'm so sorry. I'm so sorry, please . . ."

Dad can't stand it any longer. "I'm calling the police," he decides.

I sit on one of the bottom stairs, and Mabey comes down to sit next to me. I want to throw up. I never want to be one of those people on those crime shows I really shouldn't be watching, interviewed against a plain, dark background with the words *Gladys, victim's sister* appearing underneath me. That can't be me. It seems unreal to be watching Dad actually calling the actual police.

But it's real, as I can clearly hear. "Hello, I need to report a missing child. She's nine, her name is Agnes Burke . . ."

I don't want to listen to this. I can live without Mom, but I can't live without Agnes.

Dad is describing the clothes she's wearing when we hear a car pull into the driveway. The three of us run outside to see a silver minivan, driven by a gray-haired woman who looks familiar. The van door opens, and Agnes steps out, followed by my good friend Harry Homework and his brother, Anderson.

"I'm home," Agnes announces.

"She's home!" Dad drops his phone on the ground and runs to her. "Oh, thank God!"

He grabs Agnes, hugs her way too tight, and cries, as do Mabey and I. We stand there huddled in a lump, crying with relief. "We just went for ice cream," Agnes says, flabbergasted.

Dad, Mabey, and I can't stop crying. Harry and Andy look off to the side, embarrassed for us. "Hey," says Harry, waving at me without looking. I want to run over and hug him so hard for bringing Agnes home, but I'm not done hugging Agnes.

Harry's mom joins us on the lawn and introduces herself to Dad. "I'm Elena, and I'm so sorry—I didn't know you were worried about Agnes! We were doing some errands after I picked up Anderson from school, and we saw her walking along, so I honked and asked if she needed a ride . . . she said it wouldn't be a problem if we stopped for ice cream . . ."

Dad disentangles from us to shake her hand. He's breathing hard from the scare he had, but now he's laughing instead of crying. "Whoo! Elena, so nice to meet you! I'm so grateful that you gave her a ride! Whoo!" He presses one hand on his chest like he's checking to see if his heart stopped. "She's not supposed to walk home alone."

"Well, it was a pleasure having her along for the ride," Harry's mom says. "And I'm glad everything turned out all right!" Dad shakes her hand and thanks her again, still laughing like a lunatic, and she backs away, smiling politely. "Oh, it's no problem. Well, boys, we really should get home. Hope to see you soon, Agnes!"

"Whoo!" Dad tries to get his laughing under control. "Thanks again!" The Homework family piles into their minivan and departs. We stand on our front lawn and wave as they drive away.

Dad puts one arm around Mabey and one arm around Agnes. Mabey extends an arm to me, and I let her drape it over my shoulder.

Everybody's here where they should be. Our family is complete.

33

The Following Saturday

I'm sitting at a table that's covered in purple foil and draped with a bunch of Christmas lights.

Here we are: the Spring Dance.

Harry's sitting next to me, but I'm not his date. His date is on his other side: my sister Agnes, who captured Harry's heart the minute she got in his mom's minivan. In that fateful car ride/ice cream stop, they discovered their mutual love of math and science, plus seventy thousand other things they have in common. They're too young for romance, but they've become inseparable friends.

It was sweet, the way Harry told me about it on

Monday, like he didn't want to hurt my feelings. "I hope it's not too weird for you . . . me and Agnes, I mean."

I was like, "I'll try to get over it." When he came over to our house earlier today, he gave me this guilty little wave before going down to the lab with Agnes, where they did something that required all the baking soda in the fridge and caused them to laugh their butts off.

Anyway, since Harry and Agnes were going to the dance, and since Izzy was going to the dance, and since Izzy encouraged me to go because apparently these dumb things are really fun and people enjoy them, I said, "Okay, I'm going to the dance." So I'm here. And she's right. It's kind of fun. Everybody's all decked out and hyper and running around—Izzy keeps stealing the helium balloons and sucking the helium out and jabbering at people like a chipmunk, while Desiree tries to corral the surviving balloons somewhere safely away from her.

Over by the food table, Taye is talking with Jackson, aka, the Target. Taye finally confessed his feelings to his friend, and Jackson took it pretty well. He doesn't like Taye like that, but he didn't freak out or anything, and judging from the way they're punching each other in the shoulder, their friendship looks as solid as ever.

Among the people who aren't here tonight:

1. Madison Graham. She's been keeping a low profile at school, ever since Violet and Vanessa outed her as a liar and a snitch. Watching them over the past week, as they publicly tore Madison apart, I can see why she wanted a fake boyfriend—to go with her fake friends. Frankly, if that was my reality, I'd choose fantasy, too.

2. Jasmine. Her mom grounded her for the rest of her life when she found out the secret boyfriend was *seventeen years old*. The boyfriend didn't know Jasmine was

only twelve, but when he found out, he ghosted like a dead guy with a house to haunt. At least Mr. Gerber let her come back to band.

3. My friend Sophie Nelson. But not because she's hiding from the world. She's at a "healing retreat" weekend with her mom. Otherwise, she'd have been here early, helping to decorate the gym as a humble volunteer. She's not on the student council or the dance squad anymore, and people have been talking about her since they found out she'd been stealing. But Sophie's been brave about it. She's embarrassed, and it's been hard for her to watch her friends go off to dance squad without her, but she's incredibly grateful that her permanent record isn't marred for life, thanks to Carolina.

It turns out that Carolina knew about Sophie's stealing problem for a while. She didn't know how to say anything or how to help Sophie stop, but she did know how to butter up her mom and get a fat stack of cash from her, and that was super-duper short-term helpful in keeping Sophie from getting in serious legal trouble. I appreciate Carolina a lot more now, and she's grudgingly learning to appreciate me. She has no choice, now that I'm Sophie's other best friend.

Dad and Sophie's mom never wound up rescheduling their meeting. I suspect that Gloria didn't really want to start a business—she wanted to start something with Dad—but her priorities have changed since Sophie came clean. Meanwhile, Ms. Rivera clarified her dating policy to Dad—she doesn't date the parents of her *current* students. Agnes won't be her student next year.

Agnes's school lets out on June 22. I'm pretty sure Dad's planning to call Ms. Rivera on June 23.

And Mom . . . is Mom. She's not coming for a visit anytime soon. She and Dad aren't going to get back together. She's going to stay at the farm, where she can raise chickens instead of children. I don't like it, but I'm learning to accept it. In fact, I'm starting to think it might be better this way.

Mom called last night, and we chatted for a few minutes. She said she was sorry she couldn't visit like she'd planned to, but . . .

"I know," I said. "It was the timing."

Anyway. Since there's no business for me to do tonight—no missions to run, no problems to solve—I'm thinking I might join Izzy on her balloon quest, or get some more snack-ammo before the food fight starts, or, as the DJ keeps suggesting, *throw my hands in the air, and wave 'em like I just don't care.*

The gym smells like rain and daffodils tonight. I'll remember it for years to come.

Math and Science Notes from the Author

Toilet Volcano

1. Pour vinegar into toilet.
2. Pour baking soda into toilet.
3. Clean entire bathroom.

Clothes Dryer as Centrifuge

Doesn't work, will damage dryer, don't do it.

Barbecue Lighter as Flamethrower

Does work, will damage everything, don't do it.

Spontaneous Combustion
Not actually a thing.

Effects of Lightning Strikes
Totally a thing.

The Six Simple Machines
1. Lever
2. Wheel and axle
3. Pulley
4. Inclined plane
5. Wedge
6. Screw

Newton's Three Laws
1. An object at rest tends to stay at rest, and an object in motion tends to stay in motion, unless acted upon by an outside force.
2. Force = Mass × Acceleration

3. For every action, there is an equal and opposite
   reaction.

Probability of Picking a Double Domino
Yeah, I'm stumped.

Acknowledgments

Thanks to the editor and originator of this book, Wesley Adams, who came up with the idea and gave it to me. Now when people ask me, "Where do you get the ideas for your books?" I can tell them, "Wesley Adams."

Thanks also to editor Melissa Warten, who gave me excellent notes for revision; book designer of my dreams Aimee Fleck; and Joy Peskin, for bringing me into the FSG MacKids family.

Thanks ALWAYS to my husband, my shrink, my friends, and my family.

This book is dedicated to my beloved father, Larry Erlbaum. He and I both give thanks for my beloved stepmother, Sylvia.